Poised Like a Knife

& other stories of

Mystery,

Romance and Intrigue

including

Glorious Love and Legitimate Death

by

Deborah DR Kralich

Poised Like a Knife

by Deborah DR Kralich

Published by Ruskras Corner

The United States of America

ISBN 9781942542162

Table of Contents

Glorious Love and Legitimate Death

by Deborah DR Kralich

Spring 1914, a time of grace and elegance when the gentle breezes of peace lingered with great delicacy over England.

I, an all-American male embarking on the quest for adulthood, perched on the stone rim of a wishing well in an English garden of a temporarily deserted country home.

I shifted my position to strike what I hoped was a dashing pose, imagining I was a prince of the realm fresh from the hunt, resting before evening social engagements.

Reality was far more intriguing.

Although to dwell on it made butterflies in my stomach.

I was here at the request of my government as– it still took my breath away– a courier of secret documents. A most unlikely courier for I was not an agent posing as a nonchalant amiable tourist but an inexperienced terrified sightseer wondering how a secret agent behaves in the company of a confederate.

I, Anthony Clift, was almost a spy.

Almost. For I did not know what was in the documents nor why they were vital to security. Indeed I did not know how the government even knew I was planning a trip to England during the summer vacation between my sophomore and junior years at college. I would never know these things and never know other things as well.

4

It was generally known that my father, a businessman, belonged to a group of extremely pro-British Americans who were lobbying against German influence in Congress.

Just before my sailing I had been approached quietly and told as a patriotic loyal American I could be of valuable help if I would just make a short detour in the midst of my trip, pick up a pre-addressed envelope and drop it in the British mail. Then I was to continue my trip as originally planned.

I had been assured by those in charge that the chances of any trouble were almost nil. But the envelope had to be mailed at all costs.

Now awaiting the Englishman at the appointed location, I was feeling more and more like an amateur extremely out of place.

The agent was two hours late.

I was imagining him dead, splattered on the rocks of the English seacoast or smothered in the plush velvet curtains of some English manor.

Then I saw her.

She was stunning, ethereal, magnificent, all at once.

Many famous faces of the fledgling film industry would never have been had she not rebuked theatrical arts for espionage. Incredible Lily of the Nile eyes surpassed all the incubating movie stars soon to burst upon the world in silent glory.

She was a wild man's dream, gowned in floating swirls of unreachable blue sky.

This angel was flowing toward me…

As I was a standing dead man. She had to reach down to find my hand to shake it.

Out of the lips of this heavenly creature came a practical British voice.

"So awfully glad to find you still here. I'm Roselene. As you can see I've been at a formal tea. I had a wretched time of the getting away without attracting suspicion."

Her crisp speech brought me down from the clouds and I was able to move slightly and hoarsely attest to my coherence with an imbecile, "how do you do?"

Roselene, the obvious aliased angel (for I had been told real names would not be used) smiled and looked terribly sorry for me.

"Your first mission? My, they are recruiting young these days."

"I'm not," I whispered. "I mean I don't–"

"You do not have to whisper," she whispered with mock conspiracy. "There is no one around to hear us."

"I'm not an agent," I said, in normal tones. At least I hope I sounded faintly normal.

She laughed. "We are all supposed to disclaim that."

"No. I am really not," I said, as if I were discussing my career goals with my barber. "My father made it big in candy in Washington and I run one– "

"Sh-Sh." She spoke with alarm. "I am not to know anything about you."

"I forgot." I blushed, mortified at flunking basic spying the first thing.

She cut her eyes and grinned. "Big in candy, eh?"

I relaxed a little under her leniency. "Stores."

"Never heard anything. Except your code name?"

"Oh, right. Carmichael," I said, as I had been instructed.

Outwardly somewhat composed, by this time my heart was breaking inside. I had been hit squarely in the face with ice water on a hot summer day.

I could not face the thought of life without her.

She was going to turn over the papers and then I would never see her again. I would fulfill my mission, then go home, and drown myself in the Potomac. There was no other way.

She was preparing to pass the papers.

Sacrificing true love for my country, I bravely held out my hand.

At once a look of distress mingled with a trace of fear came over her indescribable features. She turned away.

"I hate to say this. But you see, there's been a bit of a complication, I'm ashamed to admit. I may need your help a bit."

A complication!

She needed my help!

I wanted to shout with hope. I might spend a moment or an hour extra with her. Perhaps even perhaps there might be some destiny in life after all.

"I am in a bit of a spot. My life as well as the papers are on shaky ground."

"What can I do? Just tell me."

"There's just one thing to do. Just one way out for me, I'm afraid."

She stopped, hesitant. Her doubt was about me, a foreigner, an amateur.

I straightened up, ready to die for her if necessary.

"What?" I barked, trying to sound as tough as a US Marine. "You've got to tell me."

With incredible poise she lifted her eyes to meet mine.

"Kill."

Several minutes passed from the time that single word fell on me until she spoke again, during which I stared so acutely at a rose that it has remained etched in my mind to this day.

"You are new. And so young. I cannot be sure but you must not be 25 yet."

I vehemently denied being less than a quarter-century old as if it were a social disgrace.

"If you want out– "

"No." I was shouting at her. "No, I do not want out."

"I could seek help elsewhere. There might still be time."

"There is not time and you know it." I was trying to reflect the doubt in her voice.

She laughed a little sadly. "I'm sunk without your help. That may be an accurate statement." Then she turned to me, her eyes beseeching. "It is not me that is important, so many others and– and England–" Her voice so crisp, snapped there.

"Listen, I may not be much. But I'm all you have. And I'm an American. Americans can do anything."

Then she kissed me, grateful tears spilling over her ivory cheeks.

I wiped them away with my fingers.

She regained her composure, a professional once more.

"I will arrange the details. We will work together."

At the same setting the following afternoon, we met again. I had spent the night in a small inn not far from the rendezvous garden.

In my dreams that previous night I had rescued Roselene from a thousand different dangers with an infinite variety of heroics. After such exhausting mental practice I felt ready to tackle the Kaiser barehanded.

"The situation has deteriorated overnight. I am not going to be able to go with you. Indeed if you do not succeed, I will be finished by tomorrow morning."

"I told you, Americans never fail." I squared my shoulders.

"Good. But you will have support available from another agent. Lady Rebecca Ashton. You will be her escort at a formal dinner party tonight. You are being passed off as her distant American relative with whom she has just become acquainted. You will meet her at the manor and, then during the meal, you will act."

I nodded mutely, waiting for more.

"You will have consommé as your first course. You will sprinkle it with a powder. After it is served, there will be a diversion. Everyone will turn away from you in the direction of the noise. You will switch your bowl with that of the person on your right."

She handed me a small packet.

I waited further.

"No questions?"

"That's all?"

"That is all. Simple, see? Think you can manage it? Remember no one must see you."

"There will be poison in my soup?"

"No, no. A harmless vegetable powder. If anyone sees you sprinkle it, abandoned the switch. Drink the soup yourself. It won't hurt you."

"What's the point of the powder?"

"Listen, your part is only to give an identifying signal. Only I know who the traitor is. As things stand I cannot even enter this house without great danger to myself and others. A great deal is at stake here. Sprinkling the vegetable powder identifies you as my cohort. To complete the process you must switch the bowls. That action identifies the traitor. Then my people will take over."

"And they will kill him?"

"The subject is a traitor to England. An enemy of free people everywhere. You must wait for the diversion. Make sure no one is looking. My people will be watching but in a manner that you cannot discern. If anyone is overtly observing you, scuttle the plan. If anyone comments, offer some explanation that it is a medicinal powder you need to aid the digestion. However, everyone should be absorbed in the action."

"I hope the diversion will be obvious."

"Absolutely. You will have no doubt. The distraction will disrupt the occasion with a bang. Harmless bang, of course."

I hoped my relief that I would not be the literal killer did not show. But I feared it did and I fell in her estimation.

"Remember, no matter who sits down to your right at that dinner, no matter who it seems to be, no matter the masquerade, this is an enemy agent, a ruthless spy, who would not hesitate to destroy you or me." She gripped my arm with deadly white fingers. "The elimination of such a traitor is not murder. This is a legitimate death."

***

I was alone with four aristocratic couples.

Lady Rebecca had not shown up.

The situation must by now be critical.

The party was at the summer home of a duke and duchess. They were a young pair, barely in their 30s, obviously in the same social circle as Roselene and the mysterious Lady Rebecca. I wondered if they were both British agents. Or perhaps just the duke. Contemporaries to all the other guests age wise, they were elevated slightly above them in social stature by the untimely death of the duke's father.

The other men were Lieutenant Colonel Sir William North, Lord Richard Allison, and Sir Edward Grover.

We had not yet been called into dinner. Segregated from the women, the men conversed solely on the topic of war. So far I had no clue as to which was the ill-fated spy, nor which was to be his murderer.

Almost invisible were servants including a solicitous butler.

The traitor could not be a servant. Servants do not eat at their masters' tables.

The butler, middle aged and nondescript, inquired if I wanted a drink.

"No." I was trying to say as little as possible.

The butler beckoned a servant to serve me anyway.

"So Donelson," said the duke, addressing me by my name for the evening. "Does Americans think there will be conflict in Europe?"

"And what will America do if war comes?" asked Lieutenant Colonel North.

Somewhat taken aback at this command to speak for all of America on the monumental issue of war, I replied after a pause, "I will be happy to serve my country if war comes."

"A war jolly well would not last long enough for America to enter it," said Edward Grover, who held some obscure post in the British government. "We would be in the Kaiser's bedroom by New Year's."

"I daresay you are right, Eddie," remarked Lord Allison.

"Quite so, don't you agree, Donelson?" asked North.

"Well."

"And yet," Lord Allison sniffed. "I hear rumblings that America may not take our side."

"Irrelevant," said North. "Why would we want them fighting with us? Sharing the glory? Armament sales are what matters."

"The Americans might be uncooperative in that vein also," suggested Allison.

They now all stared at me with accusing stone faces.

I coughed. "I'm afraid I don't know anything about politics, gentlemen."

"But Rebecca told us you live in Washington," said the duke. "Doesn't that sort of thing take up most of your time?"

"I run part of the family business." I thought of my little store with its friendly colorful atmosphere. Such a contrast to where I was now.

"Armaments?" North asked.

"I'm in confections. Candy."

"Sweets? Oh. Yes, indeed. You Americans, all business," said Lord Allison. "Money money money, the love of money, you Americans are famous for it."

"Better to make money than war. Better to make candy," I said lamely.

They all looked at me again.

The duke said lightly in a 'remember-he's-our-guest' manner, "well, well, yes. Less painful to make money. And, um, candy."

The Englishmen seem to believe this was a joke and therefore laughed.

"Where is my dear Rebecca this evening?" the duke asked Lieutenant Colonel North as if her whereabouts were of sudden vital importance. "I thought she was coming with her American relative here."

"Come to think of it, I don't know." Lieutenant Colonel North punched my shoulder and I jumped. "Hey Donelson, you know anything about her latest intrigue? I mean, what is she really up to these days? Rebecca is so secretive. She never tells her old pals anything anymore. What has she told you? There is a man in the picture? Right?"

I reviewed Roselene's instructions rapidly. She had mentioned nothing about Lady Rebecca having a boyfriend.

"Lady Rebecca never mentioned anything."

"Typical of her," said Lieutenant Colonel North.

"Do you actually call her Lady Rebecca?" asked Lord Allison with some surprise. "I mean, she is your long lost cousin I know. But even if you have not seen each other since birth or whatever, you Americans are usually so informal. I expected you would be calling her Becky or Becca or Beck or something idiotic like that."

I let myself nourish a strong hope that Lord Allison was the man marked for death.

Fortunately at that moment we were called to join the ladies.

Lady Allison was a large stout woman who said virtually

nothing all night. Lady Grover was a small birdlike woman who twittered constantly but managed to say nothing either. Lieutenant Colonel North had brought his fiancée Lady Constance who seemed the best of friends with the genial duchess.

"Call me Anne," the duchess insisted as she took my arm. "I wanted to be informal like the Americans so you will feel at home. Have the men been talking about war all evening? I imagine it must be very boring to you. Rebecca tells us any potential conflict is almost never discussed in America. The isolationists expect to keep America out of it."

"That's right." I was grateful for the friendly touch of her hand.

"Did you see Rebecca when she was in America?" asked Lady Constance.

I found myself flush. I did not know the answer to that one either. How many more unanswerable questions would there be?

"Yes." I was guessing this was the right thing to say.

"Funny," said Lady Constance. "Funny, she never mentioned it. I thought she went to New York on that visit."

"You know," said Anne. "Rebecca so different these days. She has changed so. She never calls me anymore. I used to know all her secrets. Now it's almost like she avoids me."

"We all grew up together. Went to school together. We're like sisters." Lady Constance was explaining this to me.

"You know that would make you our honorary cousin." Anne laughed so pleasantly that I felt at ease for the first time.

It seemed as if this comment was meant to provoke a salute.

"Yes. Cousin. How about it?" Lady Constance raised her drink.

"Wonderful. The honor is mine."

Anne joined in the toast.

For a moment her friendly clear eyes met mine and her smile warmed the room.

Three glasses clicked.

"And, are you boring our guest?" The duke appeared from nowhere abruptly. He spoke in an irritable manner which he seemed to reserve especially for his wife.

"No, dear, of course not." She was surprisingly defensive. "Constance raised the toast."

"Then do not monopolize him." He brusquely grabbed my arm and led me away from her. He deposited me on the other side of the room between Lady Grover and Lady Allison.

They regarded me with blank expressions.

Mercifully, dinner was called.

We walked through the white carpeted hall towards the huge dining room. A delicious aroma wafted through the doors. Servants beckoned. The huge round table was splendidly set with gleaming china and sparkling crystal. The intricately carved high-back chairs seemed more like thrones.

My head swam. Here I was at a formal English dinner party not unlike those frequented by the king and queen. In the company of important men of destiny. At least one British secret agent and a British traitor were among my dinner companions.

I was to act as betrayer to that German sympathizer, instigating his death.

The seating began. A cold chill iced my dizzy light head. And my blood froze in my veins. At English formal dinners the guests sat: man– woman – man– woman.

A woman would be to my right.

We were upon the table.

Lieutenant Colonel North took his place furthest from the door.

Lady Grover was seated.

Then the duke.

Then, Lady Allison.

Lord Grover.

Lady Constance.

I was next.

I was between the duchess and Lady Constance, the latter flanked by Lord Allison.

The duchess was to my right.

Anne. No, not Anne to me now. Once again- the duchess…

Waiters entered bearing gleaming ivory china bowls.

The chatter at the dinner table was a monotonous hum. I realized I had a terrible headache. My head pounded with the words 'legitimate death, legitimate death' repeating over and over in my brain, interspersed with bits of unforgettable phrases-

Legitimate death…

Tidbits of conversation remain with me today-

"So glad to hear the good news…"

"A ruthless despot, an enemy agent…"

"Russia will never fight Germany, you mark my words…"

"Not just myself but others in England…"

"Alexandra calls the shots there, old man…"

"Must be mailed at all costs…"

"And are you feeling quite well this time and…"

"Every hope that this time will be successful…"

"An enemy of free people everywhere…"

"My darling, I am so glad…"

Legitimate death.

There was a terrific crash from the front of the house.

Everyone appeared to turn and look away. Lieutenant Colonel North left the room.

Shortly the butler appeared in the doorway and announced that Lady Rebecca Montgomery had crashed her car into one of the huge brick gate posts.

The duke turned a ghastly white.

The consommé in white china gleamed like stars.

I focused my mind on Roselene's lovely face as I sprinkled the powder, then deftly switched the bowls.

An attempt on the life of Lady Rebecca. My mission was more urgent than ever.

Lieutenant Colonel North returned to report that Lady Rebecca was only badly shaken up. The flutters of the servants were audible as the accident victim was brought inside.

Lieutenant Colonel North left again.

Not a drop was spilt.

No one noticed.

Lieutenant Colonel North returned to report her ladyship was going straight upstairs to lie down.

And she begged to be excused for the rest of the evening.

The servant still cooed but the voice of my false cousin was too low to discern as she was hustled upstairs.

The duke relaxed.

The formal dinner continued with a new topic of discussion.

"Rebecca is going to kill herself in that automobile one day," said Lord Grover.

"You're so right, dear," Lady Grover agreed.

"We all know her. She never takes even the most simple precautions. A reckless daredevil in every pursuit in every area of her life," said Lord Allison.

"You are so correct, my dear," said Lady Allison.

And so conversation rolled on as we sampled our soup.

It was delicious.

I felt a great sense of relief at having done my part and with that came a ferocious hunger. I had hardly eaten since I had met Roselene.

The duchess beside me ate with the most delicate manners. She held the spoon as though it were an ink pen. She savored each sip as though it were poetry.

I watched each ounce rise up from her bowl.

Her exquisite lips caressed each spoonful unaware her food was enhanced with a digestive aide. An identifying signal.

I took part in the conversation as best I could, trying not to stare at her. I want to scrutinize her face as if it would reveal why she joined the other side. I wondered how much longer she would live and how she would be eliminated.

What about the others? Which of these proper social figures secretly worked alongside Roselene, trying to thwart the enemy from denigrating our democratic way of life?

Suddenly I felt terribly homesick for America. I was still experiencing a longing for an adventure but so far it was not as satisfying as I had envisioned it would be.

Home was much dearer now...

But Roselene– how could I leave without Roselene?

My thoughts were crushed by a sickening whimper from the duchess.

As pale as the china, she pushed herself away from the table, dropping her spoon with a clatter.

The rest of the diners gazed on, confused.

She stood up, her chair crashing to the floor behind her. She pointed down to the consommé bowl.

"My friends, I think I have eaten mushrooms." She staggered then, her hand pressing her waist. Lady Constance rose, crossed behind my chair, and held the duchess up.

"A doctor," said Lady Constance. "Send for a doctor!"

The butler materialized in distress.

"You fool, you idiot!" yelled Lieutenant Colonel North, temporarily forgetting his British reserve.

"You gave her mushrooms?" The duke's question sounded like mere curiosity.

"I assure Your Lordship," said the butler, in deep distress. "There were none in Her Grace's soup. I saw to it myself. It was prepared separately. The consommé recipe used only a trace of mushrooms for flavoring, not possibly enough to hurt her even if she got the wrong bowl."

No one else heard him. All gathered around the duchess who could no longer stand, even with Lady Constance's support. She was taken to the sofa. A doctor arrived rapidly and banished us all to the drawing room.

Lord and Lady Grover were preparing to leave. Lieutenant Colonel North was with the duke. The Allisons remained with Lady Constance and I.

"What's going on? What's happened to her?" I asked.

"She's deathly allergic to all mushrooms. They are deadly poison to her. Everyone knows that. All the servants wherever she eats are urgently cautioned. Here in her own home she should have had no worries," said Lady Constance.

"Won't it be just as if she has the flu?"

"She almost died from eating them before. Just one little bite

16

almost killed her when she was a child, eating from her mother's plate. That is how they knew. Children are rarely fed mushroom dishes. All her life since, such care had been taken. Now this!" Lady Constance was near tears.

"She will not die, my dear," said Lady Allison. "She's an adult now. It's much different with adults."

"Of course she won't die," said Lord Allison. "Dreadful butler. Carelessly making her feel bad. He should be shot."

Lady Constance had tears in her eyes. "You don't understand. She's expecting another child. She lost her first baby six months ago. If she gets so sick that she miscarries again so soon–"

I walked out of the room, trying to get far enough away so as not to hear anymore.

***

Roselene and I met before dawn at the same garden. We skipped a formal greeting and stood in silence for a moment. Then she wordlessly handed me the envelope.

"Post this," she said, taking a deep breath. "And it is all over."

"I'm going back to America immediately." I caressed the package, holding it like a baby. "I cannot continue my trip."

"I thought you might. That's all right."

I turned away.

"You see." She had some unfathomable regret in her voice. "I thought if you knew, you might not– anyways, who knows? I might be wrong, all wrong."

I put away all my pride and begged her desperately to come with me. I confessed without shame that I adored her, worshiped and idolized her.

I strove with all my willpower not to kneel at her feet.

A glint of intrigued uncertainty came into her eyes.

She shook her head with a slight smile.

For a moment I remembered another woman's smile.

"The duchess?" I inquired with timidity.

"It is safe to say no further action will be necessary."

The cold businesslike voice.

In Roselene's presence I could think of another only a second.

I gazed at her face trying to memorize her features. I never wanted to forget that beauty. Those Lily of the Nile eyes.

"We must say goodbye now."

Again I begged her with all my heart to forsake intrigue and come to America with me.

"It would be too dangerous for you if we ever saw one another again. Ever." She spoke with unquestionable finality.

My shoulders literally drooped.

I hung my head.

"I know you are not officially in the service, so as a token of gratitude I took the liberty of booking your passage home." She held out a folder. "Spare you the expense. It was the least I could do. You saved me."

I stiffened. I did not want pay for what I had done.

"I've already made arrangements," I lied.

"Oh, I see." She withdrew her hand. Her eyes retained the glazed uncertainty.

She walked away with a light quick step.

I felt deep despair at not having been able to offer her more out of life than a candy store.

Willpower depleted, I sobbed into the wishing well.

I mailed the vital article without difficulty that morning.

The evening paper carried news of the sudden death of the duchess with regrets.

***

Seven months later on a hot summer day in Washington I clipped another article from the daily newspaper. Not the front page story from the European warfront but a small extensively captioned picture from the society pages.

In faded black-and-white, my haunting Roselene cradled an infant in her arms, her beautiful features shielded by a thin veil.

Surrounding her were the duke, the Prince and Princess of Wales.

Read the caption-

The first child of the Duke of Burntorang
and his new bride, the former Lady Rebecca

Montgomery, was christened in London in the presence of the Prince and Princess of Wales. The baby, named Anthony, was born prematurely to the duke and duchess who were married unexpectedly this past summer soon after the death of the duke's first wife from food poisoning. The first duchess, married to the duke for a decade, was known to have a severe allergy of mushrooms, and accidentally consumed that food at the hands of an incompetent butler, who later took his life in remorse. The duke and Lady Rebecca, a close friend of the late duchess, united in grief and eloped a few days after the funeral. British society, normally eschewing such activity, rallied around the couple. The baby boy is the first child for the duke, as the late duchess was unsuccessful in her attempts to have children. The duke, a colonel in the British Army, was home from the front. He would enjoy only two weeks leave before saying farewell to his new wife and heir and return to the front in France.

***

As the many years passed I was often to read of the beautiful duchess in the news.

Her great contributions during both world wars.

Her great charitable works after the duke perished in the London blitz.

The second marriage of their only child to a popular American actress.

Her graceful recline into old age...

And always the glazed uncertainty in those Lily of the Nile eyes forcing its way through the opaque newspaper photos, stirring in me memories of wonder about glorious love and legitimate death.

Poised Like a Knife

A Lieutenant Plate in Sand Waves Mystery Short Story

by Deborah DR Kralich

Characters

Adults facing the storm:

Jacqueline Tirr- Native Houstonian, successful realtor, she chose to reside in Sand Waves. Neighbors had no alternative but to accept the novelty of a single woman buying a new house and living alone in a subdivision created for traditional family units.

Jean Carston- Homemaker and mother, new to Texas, she had quit her part-time typist job when her baby was born 2 years ago.

Mark Carston- Transplanted from New Jersey, now an analyst for Texaco, like his wife, Mark had never seen a hurricane.

Lennon Green- Her soft purring southern voice belied she was the only mother in this social set who worked at all.

Alex Green- Former Florida resident, this accountant was a hurricane veteran, now with his own firm in Texas.

Leigh Carter- Married young, childless for years, never employed. Now she had a baby to care for and worry about.

Greg Carter- Video game salesman, he had turned a poverty stricken childhood in Ohio into prosperity as an adult in Texas.

Lieutenant Sinclair Peter Plate- Young, attractive, intelligent second in command among a handful of cops in this elite community.

Children on the block:

Jenny and Sarah Green- Well-behaved 6 and 4 year old sisters.

Tyler Carter- A spoiled 2-year-old with a new kitten.

Ark Carston- The 8-month-old was frequently ill.

Pets in the families:

Bandit- Jacqueline's feline companion, as important to her as any child...

Train- The Carston family dog, usually good with children, the Carston baby was still too young to play.

Kitty- Weeks in the world, the newest arrival to this group was oblivious to the storm about to come and at the mercy of his toddler master.

Poised Like a Knife

by Deborah DR Kralich

Jacqueline went to bed at midnight after a long day of following the hurricane's advance via the new cable television phenomenon, *The Weather Channel.*

She was enjoying the novelty of not having to wait until the network news programs deigned to filter information about the impending storm. The cable weather forecasters had expected the hurricane to hit land that evening but it had stalled in the Gulf of Mexico, gaining strength. Within the tempest, swirling winds blew over 90 miles an hour, growing every minute.

But the huge treacherous mass slowed to a sluggish northeast movement and was not now expected to slam into the upper Texas coast until dawn.

The Houston Galveston area had not experienced a major hurricane in almost 20 years, not since Hurricane Carla in 1964. Since then, each season, there was a threat or two. Hundreds of miles out in the water a turbulence would form. It would travel, strengthen, hover and poise like a knife at the throat of the greater metropolitan area. But always, just as the area prepared for the worst, the storm would veer away and strike Florida or Mexico or somewhere else.

No one had expected a storm so late in the 1981 season to actually strike.

It would dissipate or turn east.

The sprawling metropolis would breathe a collective sigh of relief tinged with mild disappointment at missing all the thrills, action and excitement. The news hungry TV crews would dejectedly disassemble their hurricane command posts. Their reporters, panting for close-ups of themselves risking life and limb on the Galveston seawall as 200 mile-an-hour winds ripped them bald, would return to their mundane coverage of Houston's daily rapes and murders. This year, Jacqueline believed the storm was coming. This time was going to be different.

This time it looked like there was no avoiding it.

The storm was large enough to affect the entire area.

And of this area, Galveston Island could be considered the head, greater Houston the body, and the small command design colony of Sand Waves the throat.

No matter which direction the storm went Sand Waves would be struck.

Local TV weather forecasters began to drool.

That morning Jacqueline had canceled all pending showings, dropping into the supermarket for candles and batteries, beating the evening rush hour crowd.

The more scientific minded had commenced marking the hurricane tracking charts printed on grocery store paper bags. Upon return Jacqueline had tossed her purchases aside, focusing on the packaging, pen and rule ready. But soap operas reduced local alerts to a tiny box in the corner of the screen, prompting Jacqueline to switch to the cable channel, abandoning the local news programming of her hometown for the first time.

A successful real estate agent, she had recently bought a new house in the command design colony called Sand Waves. Her neighbors were exclusively young married couples, husbands on the corporate rise. The majority had transferred to Houston from out of state. Most wives had preschool children and no financial need to work.

Her closest three neighbor couples, all in their late 20s like Jacqueline, fit this pattern perfectly. Jacqueline had a corner house and next door lived Alex Green, CPA, and his wife, Lennon, with two daughters Jenny, six, and Sarah, four.

Directly across the street from Jacqueline were Jean and Mark

Carston. Mark was an analyst for Texaco. Jean had quit her part-time typist job when their first baby was born eight months ago.

On the other side of the Carstons, directly across from the Greens, lived Greg and Leigh Carter. A salesman, Greg married Leigh when they were both very young. She had never been employed. Their spoiled two-year-old was named Tyler.

The three couples had become friends. Often in the evening they could be found in one of their front yards chatting as their children played.

Jacqueline would sometimes unfold her lawn chair and join them a while. But she considered them all terribly sweet and hopelessly dull. She saw them as carbon copies of one another. Plastic vanilla families, remnants of 1950s TV sitcoms, living the upper middle-class American dream of that era, when true love was found in college and success was measured by congruences.

They appeared beyond the reach of life's imperfections that Jacqueline, as a single career woman, knew so well. Their twilight discussions centered on the focal point of their domestic lives- their children.

Jacqueline, having a compelling need to spend all her time expediently, had no moments to spare for leisurely conversation detailing parentage. She would soon make her excuses and leave.

With the storm nearing, each couple had kindly invited her to spend the night with them, thinking that she would be afraid to be alone.

She refused politely, shaking her head at the idea that anyone could bear to be anywhere but home when a hurricane struck.

For the previous two days the subdivision had been under a deadly hot calm. A hurricane watch.

"So you think the storm is coming?" Jean had said to Jacqueline that first day of the watch. They had all been lounging in Jean's yard that evening. The Carstons, from New Jersey, had never been through a hurricane.

"These watches can go on for days and days," said Alex. Being from Pensacola, the Greens were hurricane veterans.

"Oh, indeed," agreed Lennon in her soft purring southern

voice. "Days."

She was keeping an eye on their daughters who were bicycling in the street. Lennon was the only working mother of the three in any fashion, handling details of her husband's accounts for him.

"They say we are long overdue for a storm in this part of Texas," Jacqueline said with relish.

"Do you remember the last one? No! No, Train!" Jean reached and grabbed her dog by the collar. Train, a huge well-disciplined German Shepherd was hungrily eyeing Tyler's new kitten.

The kitten barely a month old was crouching warily under Lennon's lawn chair.

"It was bad," Jacqueline said, hoping to impress and not mentioning she had been only four. "I remember sleeping on a mattress in the floor for days."

"Why sleep on a mattress?" asked Greg.

"My parents put it under an open window for me so I would sleep a little cooler. There was no electricity for weeks."

"No air conditioning!" cried Mark, in mock horror. "We will have to leave for Acapulco immediately."

Laughing he grabbed Jean in a playful hug. She laughed with him, her long Scandinavian blonde hair swinging as he held her. Their dog nuzzled them both in a charming picture of family affection. "Good boy!" The canine was praised by both his owners.

"You joke," Jacqueline said. "Just wait when it is 98 at 6 PM and drops, oh maybe all the way to 89 at midnight, and you have no air conditioning, or refrigerator. Or possibly, even no running water. You'll be ready to leave for Alaska."

"How will that affect your baby?" Leigh asked. She had a plaintiff whiny voice even when she was not complaining.

"Hopefully, not too bad," said Mark. Infant Ark Carston had recently been quite ill. He had been hospitalized for a few days but had come home the previous day.

"He'll be okay," said Jean, sobering as she glanced at her baby who was in his pram. Tyler was running around and around the stroller, Indian fashion, emitting a hooting sound. The baby watched fascinated. Train started to join in. "Train! Stop that! Good boy,

Train. "

"If it is too bad, we'll go somewhere where there are lights and get a motel room." Mark grabbed the dog and petted him again.

Time for me to leave, thought Jacqueline. *We've got to the kids.*

"I hope none of my trees come down," Jacqueline said, in an effort to get the conversation back to the storm.

Everyone automatically gazed upward at the towering trees in their own yards.

Sand Waves was sprinkled with tall pines and ancient oaks. The developers advertising slogan was 'The Inhabitable Forest'.

"There's nothing to do about it if it does," said Alex.

Sand Waves had already experienced a tornado that summer. The funnel cloud had touched down a few blocks over, sending several trees smashing into cars parked on driveways. One had landed on a house tearing a gaping hole in the roof.

"I just hope the storm won't hit here," said Leigh. "I'm afraid of the emotional effect on Tyler at his age."

The other mothers exchanged glances. Leigh was considered an overprotective mother. And Greg saw his only son as a potential president- of a corporation if not the country.

The Carters were from Ohio. Leigh had once confided to Jacqueline that Greg came from a poor family. He had made good selling videogame equipment. Upon his success he had completely broken with his illiterate family, who all drank a great deal. He had married Leigh, a dentist's daughter, and was a strict convert to middle class domesticity.

"I just hope we don't have any flooding," Alex was saying.

"Our houses are not in the floodplain, but that doesn't mean anything here," Jacqueline said.

"Flooding does the most damage," said Lennon. "At least it does in Florida."

She rose and stretched.

"Girls," she called, "it is time to go in for supper."

Then a dreadful thing happened.

When Lennon rose, the normally quiet dog yielded to his

instincts and dove for the kitten. Without the least fear of the familiar dog, and frantic to protect his kitten, Tyler ran between them. The cat arched his back and hissed. The dog snapped.

Leigh screamed and Greg went deathly pale as blood appeared on Tyler's shoulder. Instinctively Greg grabbed the dog and pulled him back.

The boy cried in pain and betrayal. Mark and Jean wrestled their dog from Greg and forced him to the ground as if they were competing in a calf scramble. Sobbing, Leigh clutched her child, causing him to yell louder.

Upon relinquishing the dog, Greg haphazardly attempted to pry his wife off Tyler, all the while repeating his son's name over and over.

Lennon, the most experienced mother, recovered her wits first.

"Let's see." She gently coaxed the frightened Leigh to let go. She cradled Tyler and he relaxed. "Oh, it's just a scratch. Just take him for tetanus and he'll be okay." In her calm hands, Tyler's scream deteriorated to a whimper. "I don't even think you'll need stitches."

Jean and Mark let the German Shepherd go. He scampered off, happily unaware of any misbehavior. Jacqueline looked around for the kitten. It had disappeared. She was grateful Bandit never came outside.

"Come on," said Mark. "I'll take you to the emergency room. We'll pay the charges."

And thus broke up the neighborhood gathering.

The second day Jacqueline had taken off from work to prepare for the coming storm. It was now 90 miles southeast of Galveston moving in a West Northwest pattern. Experts were still unsure the point of landfall but Galveston Island was a safe bet. Jacqueline counted candles, flashlight batteries, and made sure her non-electric clocks were ticking. She decided against taping the windows. During the last hurricane threat she had taped her apartment windows and when she vacated the place two years later, the gum was still clinging to the glass. And that hurricane never made it to Houston.

But she made sure there was no debris in the yard. As she was dragging in the waterhose, she waved at Lennon who was carting her potted plants into safety.

"Hey, did Tyler get all right?"

"Yes." Lennon came to Jacqueline's driveway. "I talked to Leigh late last night. He is fine. I haven't seen them this morning though. Jean's baby is sick again."

"Really?"

"Yeah, how about that. Darn it, I guess he had a relapse."

"Did they take him back to the hospital?"

"I think they took him to the doctor. I don't know if they put him back in."

"I see." Jacqueline trudged on into the garage. She dumped the hose and scooped up her two-year-old calico cat, who called the attached garage home. The feline with black markings across her eyes perfectly simulating a mask spent a good percentage of time in with Jacqueline when her mistress was not working. But she was a reclusive kitty who preferred to be alone most of the time.

"Bandit, in the house you go. In there you will stay with me until this passes."

She put the feline through the door. Then after pulling the car into the garage, she opened the freezer. Two pork chops and three pounds of hamburger would spoil. She put them in the oven to cook slowly. As soon as they were done, she would freeze them cooked. They would keep longer that way. That done, she would be ready for the hurricane. She set her alarm clock for 6 AM.

She awoke to a strange buzzing. She fingered her Touch-on lamp. Dead. The electricity was already off. Frogs were screaming. Birds were silent except for a coo coo coo every 30 seconds. She reached for her flashlight and hung her head down. She peered upside down under the bed. Bandit was hunched on all fours, eyes wide open. Groggily, Jacqueline stumbled into the living room. Out her huge living room windows she could see no wind. But it was coming. The dawn was cloudy. Her ears popped as though in a diving airplane. Low barometric pressure. She peered up at her front yard trees, one tall pine, two large oaks, and three moderate sweet gums.

"Hang in there, trees," she said idiotically.

She could see both the Carston and the Carter front yards. There was a huge oak tree right on their property line between side-by-side drives. On her side of the street the old oak, like the others carefully preserved by the developers as to better market the subdivision, was on her side of the property line she shared with the Greens.

Not that the tree knows it is mine and should not fall on the neighbor's house, Jacqueline thought with a smile. Old oaks were infamous for uprooting in hurricanes. Tall pines snapped. Two or three feet up the trunk.

Mark and Jean had left one of their cars out of the garage.

"Stupid Yankees," Jacqueline thought unkindly, still half asleep. But then she remembered they had a sick child. A car could be trapped in the garage as easily as it could be smashed by a tree in the drive.

They could all be trapped in the subdivision if Galveston Bay flooded.

"Good heavens!" She spoke to Bandit who had come to look at the window with her. It became harder to see. Rain was beginning to fall.

From behind Jean's car, which partially blocked the view of the Carter garage, the Carter's garage door was manually raised. Greg came into view carrying what looked like a large fat briefcase and walked around towards his car's trunk. *Surely he doesn't think he's going to work.*

Walking down the drive in the direction of his mailbox, Greg appeared to gaze right at her, despite the downpour.

Jacqueline backed away from the window a little, since she was not dressed. She grabbed a robe and peeked out again. Greg had not backed his car out of the garage. His back to her now, he strode quickly back towards the house. Apparently he had changed his mind.

Jacqueline was pleased with herself that she had gathered her mail in plenty of time to avoid getting wet.

She went into her bathroom and checked the water. It was still on. Better take a quick bath before it went off or became contaminated. The hot water heater would still hold a warm reserve.

She turned on the faucet. Water rushed noisily into the tub. Bathing by candlelight, she heard a splatter of rain hit the roof.

Bandit began to claw the bathroom door.

"Meowo wow!" screamed Bandit. The wind echoed her cry.

"It's all right," Jacqueline said to her frightened pet, letting her in to witness her mistress' bath.

She played with the kitty's ears as she relaxed in the warm water.

When the water started to cool, she dressed and came out. The house was now much lighter, for technically it was now daytime. Jacqueline pulled open her living room curtains. The front yard trees were dancing in the air. The brunt of the wind was coming southeast, hitting her house squarely in the face.

She ran to the back door which was composed of little glass rectangles bordered by narrow strips of wood.

A French door had seemed like such a good idea when she had selected the design…

Each little rectangle was ready to burst if a tree limb came shooting through. The unsold house behind her was fully completed but still builder owned. Jacqueline had watched them tack the carpet had only a week ago. She had taken the workers some cold drinks as they labored in the hot house, forbidden to turn on the air as they worked.

A huge oak tree dominated this backyard with a smaller sweet gum beside it. Jacqueline watched with amazement as two limbs, one oak and one gum, literally tied themselves into a hard knot. The wind and rain were now blowing in sheets so hard that each gust sounded like an 18 wheeler speeding down her side street.

Jacqueline knew it was time to take Bandit and hibernate in the windowless guest bathroom.

But the thrill of the storm captivated her.

For better or for worse, she had to watch.

She switched on her transistor radio. Above the cracking and popping, the announcer rasped that the storm was raking through Galveston with the eye headed towards Houston. She turned the radio down.

She wanted to hear the pure sounds of the storm.

Bandit raced from window to window in a nervous trot. Jacqueline followed the cat, mentally calculating where each tree might fall.

One oak threatened the attached garage at the front. Another leaned over the dining room and still another could easily crush her front porch alcove. Her backyard pine trees were flush against the protective western wall, thus safe from the southeastern winds except for their tops.

Now the front yard trees bent at right angles towards the Carston house as though they had rubber trunks. At last check, the two trees behind her were still spectacularly entangled, their glistening branches resembling an intricate masterpiece of brown blown glass.

From her living room window, she watched Alex and Lennon's lone front yard pine stoop and rise as if it were exercising. The wind puffed around the naked corner of their house like smoke signals sent sideways.

Above the zizzing wind, she heard a small snap. She raced to the back door thinking the entangled limbs had broken off. Instead both trees had uprooted, smashing into the empty house. Rain poured through jagged hole in the roof.

She ran back to her front windows. Her own trees were holding on. She peered through the inundation at the Carston car. It was still there. Then she gripped the curtains. Something moved in the car.

Did her eyes deceive her or was Train in the car?

Then the rain splashed at her, coating the window. And for a second the scene was clear and magnified. And she saw.

Jean's blonde hair moving back and forth across the windshield.

Jean was in the car.

Idiot, thought Jacqueline. *She can't go anywhere in this.*

Jacqueline opened her front door and stepped onto the small porch which was shielded in an alcove. Nevertheless, rain splattered her.

"Jean!" she screamed uselessly. "Jean, get in the house!"

Tree limbs and leaves and pine needles blew past the porch.

She heard the loud cracking of wood. In alarm, she wrenched her eyes from the car to her trees. Which one? The cracking became sharper.

But it was to her left.

With horror she turned back to the car. Her neighbor's property line oak tree leaned precariously over the small auto. In wonderment she stared as Jean began to beat the windshield.

Why doesn't she get out? Jacqueline thought- then at the same moment- *she can't.*

Jacqueline ran into the wind, feeling the rain pelting her like pepper shot.

Struggling to keep her balance, she sprinted the short distance across the yards.

Pure terror on her face, Jean's mouth worked with frantic screams drowned by the rampage. She pounded on the glass with both fists, her body moving awkwardly back and forth inside the small car much as Bandit had fled from window to window in the house. Jacqueline jerked the car door handle. Nothing happened.

"Unlock the door!" Jacqueline screamed.

Then she saw Jean holding up a little lever that unlocked the door from the inside. Jacqueline ran to the passenger side of the car. The handle moved but the door would not open. It was jammed. Dents all along the side had crumpled into immobility. Frantically Jean kicked and Jacqueline pushed. But they did not have the strength between them to free the door.

Through the corner of her eye Jacqueline saw Tran draped across the back seat. His side bloodied, his eyes opened, the dog was obviously dead. But Jacqueline could not let her mind linger on a dog right now.

Crack, crack, crack went the tree,

A hammer. I must get a hammer.

She made a fist and hit her other fist with it against it to communicate with the trapped woman.

Jean nodded slightly, her blue eyes pleading and begging.

31

Crack went the tree.

She quickly assessed going back to her own house and hunting for a device to break the car glass would take longer than summoning help on this side of the street where able-bodied men were sure to have tools at hand.

Jacqueline ran beyond the endangered car to the Carston front door and pounded. Where was Mark?

He did not answer.

She sprinted behind the automobile, across the narrow driveway divide and beat on Greg's door.

The wind sounded louder.

No answer.

Crack, crack. Crack

Jacqueline had no choice now. She ran towards her own home. Running against the wind was like swimming upstream in a raging river. She finally reached her driveway when a splitting crack caused the ground to vibrate under her feet.

Jacqueline turned and saw the whole picture, staring at the Carston drive across the street for what seemed like hours.

Hanging over the car, one of its huge sloping branches poised in the air above the car in position to stab through the roof, the giant oak tree began the final breaking.

The tree, in defiance of the storm, leaned over into the wind as the air currents swirled around to push it further and crack, crack, crack sounded again.

As she gaped, Jacqueline absentmindedly let the wind nudge her backwards like a cow walks it calf.

The ancient oak tree just dipped downward, dying with grace. The sword-like branch first brushed the top of the car gently. Then the smaller spindly sticks broke off and flew away as the thick limb stabbed through the heart of the car. The weight of the full tree came after, crushing the automobile with one swift drop, like a crane whose spring had snapped. The wind chose that second to scream loudly and the crushing tree sounded to Jacqueline much like dry kindling split on a nice fall day.

Dazed, soaked, and violently shaking, Jacqueline made it to

her front door. Bandit greeted her with a confused meow as though questioning the wisdom of her mistress's foray into the whirlwind.

Jacqueline picked up her phone. After a second, a dial tone hummed reassuringly. She dialed the Sand Waves emergency number, which she had memorized upon purchasing her house.

Next year Sand Waves was to be incorporated into the new 911 system instituted in Houston the previous year, 1982. But it had not reached unincorporated suburbs yet.

"This is a recording," came high-pitched voice. "We have an emergency situation… Please do not tie up the lines unnecessarily. Unless this is a storm related emergency involving illness, injury or death, please hang up. Otherwise, your call will be answered by the next available officer."

Then the machine put her on hold.

***

The air was cold. The wind still whipped occasionally. Suddenly a splat of rain would pelt the ground, but oddly in the east a ray of sunlight peeked.

The eye of the storm was over Sand Waves.

Around the crushed car, a drenched quintet huddled, Jacqueline, Lennon, and Alex, Greg, and Lieutenant Plate of the Sand Waves Police Department. Further back several other residents who were only vaguely familiar or actual strangers hovered, speaking in hushed whispers.

"Tell me what happened, Ms. Tirr," said the policeman, a slim man whose solid manner and advanced rank belied his youth.

Jacqueline told him over the buzz of the chainsaws. Plain faced men in white jumpsuits converged to free Jean from the wreckage and take her away.

"A tragic accident," Greg said. He was pale white.

"Unbelievable," said Lennon. "What was she doing in the car?"'

"And that big of an oak tree snapping!" said Alex. "I never heard of such a thing."

"We're going to get her out while the eye is over us. We have maybe 10 or 15 minutes," said the lieutenant. He walked to the far side of the tree and ran his hand over the wide crack in the truck."

"Anyone know if Mark has been notified?"

"I'm waiting to talk to Mr. Carston," said the lieutenant. "He was staying at the hospital with their son while his wife stayed here with the dog. So I understand. He is however on his way here now and he should make it before the storm resumes. The freeways are still clear enough."

Alex spoke with authority. "They would be. The flooding comes after, when the rivers and bayous start to swell."

The bereaved husband arrived back in his neighborhood. The other men went to greet him as he got out of his car. The activity in his front yard necessitated his remaining outside of his own property until it concluded. Alex offered him privacy, holding out his front door key.

Mark declined. He made it was clear he wanted to stay outside with his friends as EMTs removed the body of his wife from his front yard.

"Don't hold anything back," he told the group. "I want to hear everything."

"Jacqueline witnessed the accident and tried to help," said Lennon.

As they widened their circle Mark took a place with his back to the ongoing activity. "I petitioned to cut the tree down last year and the community association vetoed it. I'm going to sue them."

"I don't blame you. No telling how old that tree is," Greg said.

Lieutenant Plate interrupted that conversation thread to introduce himself to Mark and offer his sympathies.

Mark seem to be suppressing his emotions. He wanted more facts about his wife's death.

Lieutenant Plate explained what he knew, which Mark immediately characterized as an inadequate explanation as to why his wife's body was still in the car.

"Are they going to finish before the storm returns?"

"I think so. They're almost done, Mr. Carson. I will need to speak with you after the hurricane passes. If you would write your contact information and this card, I would appreciate it."

"I want to know if this could've been prevented." Mark scribbled on a small piece of paper and handed it back to Plate.

"There will be a thorough investigation when the emergency subsides."

"I want someone from the forestry service or the agriculture service whoever has authority of in this state to determine whether that tree was a potential deathtrap in a storm like this, and my wife might not have died if I had been allowed to cut it down. The second part of the storm is liable to compromise the evidence. Can anything be done about that?"

"I took some pictures. The tree trunk had a smooth break," Lieutenant Plate said. "The tree is so large I don't think it could be blown away. And all the evidence is already wet."

"Did anybody see anything? Did anybody see it happen?"

"Would you mind repeating just exactly what you told me for Mr. Carson's benefit?" Lieutenant Plate requested of Jacqueline.

Jacqueline told her story again.

Mark showed emotion for the first time at the idea that his wife was trapped and saw her death coming but had no way to escape.

"I tried," said Jacqueline. "I couldn't get her doors open. I couldn't break the glass. I couldn't get her out."

"Thank you for trying." Mark spoke brusquely, his feelings suppressed once more.

"Did any of you see anything else?" Lieutenant Plate asked the others as Jacqueline finished.

Previously he had let Jacqueline's account stand unquestioned. Now that Mark was on the scene he seemed to want more details. He did not get them.

Alex and Lennon shook their heads.

"How about you?" He turned to Greg. "Or your wife?"

"My uh, son has been running a slight fever since morning. We've been engrossed in him. And of course, in the storm- I, uh-stayed home from work today. Because of that."

"Most everyone stayed home today," said Plate.

"I certainly wasn't going to work," said Alex.

"It's a good thing you changed your mind, Greg. I saw you

35

come out with your big briefcase this morning," said Jacqueline.

"Of course, I had to report in," Plate said.

"I hope your baby is doing okay."

"He would've been released from the hospital today but for the hurricane. They delayed the release until the morning. He is fine."

One of the technicians approached the group and addressed Lieutenant Plate. "We have finished."

Mark was offered the opportunity to view Jean's body. He declined.

"Just let me know what I have to do. I don't want to see her mangled."

"I think it best that you just take refuge from the storm for the next couple of hours. Your wife's body will be taken to the nearest county morgue. Wait until the storm passes before following. We will contact you. There's nothing you can do right now."

"I cannot even get back to my son at the hospital I presume. Fortunately his grandparents are with him there."

The EMTs drove away with Jean.

Alex offered Mark shelter if he did not want to return to his own house but he declined.

The conversation stalled.

The peripheral onlookers had wandered away. Jacqueline glanced at her oak tree nearest the garage.

The ground around it was swollen, the roots pulled loose. Still standing.

"I thought these massive oak trees could withstand anything," Jacqueline said. "My oak tree must be just as old."

"Strange," murmured Lennon. "The tree fell against the wind."

"Killer hurricanes can wipe a landscape clean."

"That may be true, Lieutenant. But this is barely a category one. It's going to cause sporadic damage, here and there, at random." Alex's experience was unquestioned.

Jacqueline replied to Lennon. "Against the wind is correct. Funny how such a thick oak snapped."

Lieutenant Plate looked sharply at Jacqueline as if what she said displeased him.

"A tornado," he said. "The winds swirled. Anything can go any way."

"I'm suing. We were never warned of the dangers when we chose this subdivision. We could have bought a house in West Houston where it's more like a prairie and new houses don't have any trees nearby."

"I almost moved there. The builder had a house exactly like the one I bought." Greg glanced at his two-story. It was the highest price floor plan on the block.

"With no trees, right? And just as close to downtown Houston."

"There were no trees. I was afraid the lack of shade would cause my light bill to be twice as high in the summer."

"It would have."

"Who cares about light bills? I apologize, Jacqueline. I'm not trying to be rude to you."

"Greg, we all understand."

"Jacqueline, don't you want to ride out the rest of the storm with us?" asked Alex.

"Jacqueline," Greg said. "I insist you come with me."

"We'd love to have you."

Mark stared at the ground almost as if pondering whether to make an offer as well.

Jacqueline firmly put a stop to their solicitations.

"No, I couldn't. I couldn't leave my cat."

"I need to talk with Jacqueline just a little more," Lieutenant Plate said. "Best thing you folks can do is just go on inside and look after your own property and families."

Mark accepted more condolences before everyone acted on that advice. Again he declined company, explaining he wanted to be alone in the house that he and Jean had shared before having to face bringing his son home from the hospital.

"I know he's just a baby. He is going to know something is different."

Lennon moved to embrace Mark but he turned away.

As her neighbors scattered, Lieutenant Plate took Jacqueline by the arm and led her into her house.

"I want you to tell me again just what you saw. Everything you saw this morning."

Jacqueline acquiesced. When she finished, Lieutenant Plate said, "I want you to think. Has everything seemed normal between Mr. and Mrs. Carston recently? Any gossip about marital trouble lately?"

Puzzled and a little disturbed, she asked why.

Lieutenant Plate paused for a moment

"I suspect this might be more than it seems." He spoke slowly as though the pace of his sentence might somehow lessen the impact of the words.

Jacqueline's eyes widened. "But- " She began to protest.

"The way that she was trapped in the car. The dents and the broken lock."

"You mean you think- ?"

"And the smooth break in the trunk."

"Mark?"

"I don't know. I may be wrong. I know huge oaks aren't likely to snap. But they do sometimes. But the way you said she was caught- well, listen this is just me talking right now and I may be way off base. Still if Carston returns and comes here and wants to talk to you, don't let him in. Say the police have instructed you not to discuss what you saw with anyone just yet. And you don't want to risk slipping up in that respect. Okay?"

"I see," said Jacqueline as she tried to picture Mark cold-bloodedly sealing Jean in the car. "But how could he make sure the tree would fall on her?"

"If he knew for certain the storm was coming, he could notch and slice the tree. He could get it to fall anywhere he wanted."

"But how would he know for sure the hurricane was coming through here?"

"That's the problem."

"Could he have some superior knowledge of the weather forecast the rest of us don't receive?"

Plate contemplated. "I don't see how."

"Maybe he knows someone high up in the weather bureau. Sort of like insider trading at the stock market."

"I honestly don't know if that is even possible. Days, weeks would be needed to prove such a scenario. If it could be proven."

"So he might get away with it."

"Look, I shouldn't be telling you all this... But if this was murder, the killer took a lot of precautions to make it look like an accident and you just about wiped out all his effort. I'm hoping that by speaking to you in private it will be noted you have already had the opportunity to tell me if you saw anyone acting suspiciously, thereby eliminating any necessity of silencing you. On the other hand, if he thinks Mrs. Carston managed to say anything to you and you haven't realized it yet or, well, people tend to be trusting of familiar faces and I just want you to be on your guard. And with this emergency, I don't have anyone to protect you."

"Yes. I see."

Within minutes after the policeman left, the wind grew.

The house darkened. The second half of the tempest promised to be blacker than the first. Bandit resumed her pacing from window to window.

Jacqueline no longer had any interest in watching the winds. She hovered near a small candle in her dinette thinking about Jean and Mark.

Apparently behind the TV commercial perfect front, darker shadows loomed. It was hard to believe but there seemed little other explanation for the broken lock and jammed door. One of the two might have been possible, but both?

And Mark murdering his wife, knowing for several days a hurricane was coming from the weather forecasts. Then fixing the tree so as to fall on her. But what if the storm had gone the other way as so many had done in the past?

Well, he could just cut the tree down...

Jacqueline frowned. She dropped her head on the table. Suddenly tired, she closed her eyes, involuntarily relaxing.

Jean's image sprang before her.

Jean's flailing arms inside the car.

Jean's limp arms dangling as the chainsaw buzzed its way to her mangled body. Jacqueline popped up.

Outside the wind and the rain screamed on. But Jacqueline could only hear the buzzing that had awakened her at the beginning of this very long day.

She felt suddenly weak and nauseated. She jerked to her feet, rushing to the phone on the bar. No comforting dial tone came this time.

She pushed the button several times. The phone was dead.

She started searching for her car keys. She needed to get away. Alone in a house without electricity or phone service, she was in great danger. Where were the damn keys? She would have to disconnect the automatic garage door opener, another useless electrical appliance, in order to get her car out. But first she had to find the keys. She searched the living room with a flashlight.

A voice called. "Jacqueline. Jacqueline? Are you in there? Open the back door."

Jacqueline stopped dead still and listened very hard.

"Jacqueline, open up. I need to talk to you."

She had enough presence of mind to hold onto the flashlight as she ran to the front door. Through the peephole she saw her front yard trees bent double again. The path to her neighbor's house seemed as inaccessible as the road to Shangri-La.

"Jacqueline, let me in. Can you hear me?"

Jacqueline ran to the hallway. She pulled down the disappearing staircase to the attic and climbed up with difficulty. She managed to pull it up behind her just as she heard a window break.

In the attic the sounds of the onslaught were amplified. She searched with the flashlight for some tool, some weapon. Then she snapped it off when she heard the stairway creaking as it went down again. She crouched in the darkest part of the attic and prepared to strike with the light. That was the only chance she had.

"I only came to get you. We want you to come stay with us."

She heard the ladder groan with his weight.

"Jacqueline, are you up here? I know you must be. Come on out now." Greg sighed deeply and flicked a cigarette lighter on.

"There you are."

He smiled a little.

"Don't hurt me," Jacqueline said. He was about 15 feet away.

He sighed deeply again. "I don't want to. Believe me, I haven't a thing against you. You've always been real nice."

"You killed Jean." Jacqueline inched backwards as she spoke, saying what came to mind. "Why? Were you having an affair?"

"You women," he said, his voice becoming nasty with disgust. "Can't you imagine anything else? What would I have wanted with her? She is the same garden variety upper class wench as Leigh."

"Then why did you kill her?" Jacqueline was guessing she was over the garage now. She could think of no way out. There was no access to the garage from the attic.

"I wasn't going to kill her. I was just going to kill that animal of hers that bit my son. Just the damn dog. They think as much of that damn dog as they do their own kid. No consideration for other people. They let their damn dog bite my son."

Greg's voice it taken on a high pitched strain.

"You'd think they'd both be at the hospital with their child, But hell no! The baby's mother has to come back to stay with the dog! I didn't even know Jean was home. I broke the back door and knifed the dog. She came out of the bedroom! High-class Yankee bitch! She screamed at me and threatened me. I tried to frighten her. She was going to call the police! As long and as hard as I work to fit in, to make, to it live out here in a place like Sand Waves! She's going to have me arrested for killing a damn dog."

In her movement backward, Jacqueline stumbled and felt the soft sting of insulation on her legs.

"Oh no," he said, advancing forward, looming like a giant. "You're not going anywhere."

Then there was a tremendous crash. Wind hit her in the face. Boards snapped and split and leaves and branches crashed all around her. She grabbed onto a rafter which miraculously held up. The oak jammed into the roof. From a gaping hole in the front of the garage roof, she could see the street. She made for the opening, scratching her arms on bark and brushing against splinters with her legs. She pulled herself out onto the roof, hugging the shingles. The wind tried hard to pry her loose. On her belly she crawled towards the flatter back of the roof.

Suddenly arms grabbed her around the waist and she screamed blindly envisioning once again the terrified hunted look of Jean as she was trapped in the little car.

Then the arms turned her over and she found herself breathing into the welcome windburnt face of Lieutenant Plate.

***

The storm had cleared downtown Houston and was finishing up in Sand Waves. Jacqueline and Lieutenant Plate were walking slowly down the street, stargazing at the smashed houses and crushed cars with little puddles of people gathered around them. Limbs and pine straw still occasionally spurted across the lawn like de-tailed tails and puffs of wind hit the ground. Murdered trees robbed of their right to die slowly, standing in the earth, had scattered their damaging debris with vengeance.

"They say one in five homes in Sand Waves has a tree on it, or worse, in it." Lieutenant Plate had completed a long conversation on his car radio after Greg had been taken away and was commenting on the resulting information.

"No deaths reported yet."

"Except Jean," Jacqueline said, as she scanned her street.

For every tree that had fallen, 10 had survived but where they had once all stood with picturesque uprightness, proudly guarding the fine new homes so recently constructed beneath them, many were now slanted or bent. Numerous trunks that were left straight sprouted twisted gnarled branches stripped naked of their leaves.

Jaggedly broken limbs hung by threads, straight down like plastic Christmas icicles. The once wholesome landscape would be tainted for a generation by the deadly assault of the storm.

"Jean Carston won't be classified as a hurricane fatality," said Lieutenant Plate.

"Imagine how angry she was when she woke up this morning and found Greg killed her pet," Jacqueline said, thinking of Bandit, realizing with pain that the cat had escaped during the excitement.

"She should have been scared, " said Lieutenant Plate. "Back in Ohio, Carter was wanted on a 10-year-old assault charge. Grounds for corporate dismissal no matter what the circumstances. When she came out of her bedroom, he saw his nice home, job, and lifestyle whipping on out with the hurricane."

"So he hit her?"

"Yes. Knocking her out. He probably could've gotten out of it right there with no more than a small charge or lawsuit. That he had been clean for 10 years, had built a new life for himself and had a family, would probably have gotten the old assault charge dropped. But she got mad. And he panicked."

"I didn't realize that day that he was so angry that Train bit Tyler, especially after Tyler was all right."

"Carter probably planned to dump the dog in a bayou or somewhere, thinking the torrent would've washed it away. With Jean's body that was too risky. He hit on the rather clever idea of putting her in her own car, putting it under the tree in her own driveway. Sawing the tree so it would fall in the storm was no gamble at all. And he was so sure she would die from the crushing tree he neglected to kill her or even bind her. His only worry was that she might come to and get out of the car. So he sealed her in. That was easy."

"Doesn't sound easy."

"Break one lock from the inside and jam the other door with a sledgehammer. It was his bad luck you discovered that. No physical evidence of it survived the crash. All I would have had to go on was a smooth break in the tree."

"I guess I actually saw him finishing up that morning."

"You did. The only time anyone could have been sure the storm was coming was just before it hit. That's what let Mark out. He was at the hospital."

"And she woke up, trapped in a car on a stormy deserted street. If I'd only been able to find something heavy or just had a little more time I could have broken the windshield."

"You can't help that. Windshields are not made to shatter easily."

"Why did you come back?"

"Carter's record. Mark Carston's alibi. And then I was struck about what you said to Carter about his big briefcase in the rain. A small power saw carrying case might look a lot like a big briefcase across the yard."

"That's what made me realize Greg had killed her," said Jacqueline. "This morning I woke to a buzzing. Just before I saw him. I thought my alarm clock sounded different. The clock never really went off at all. The electricity was already out. The buzzing was the chain saw, powered by gasoline."

"Another thing that let Carston out, in my mind," said Lieutenant Plate, "was the Carston baby. What man would kill a wife with an infant baby? I certainly would not want an infant in diapers on my hands. I'd wait until the kid was a little older to kill my wife. If I had one." He grinned.

They had made the block and were back at her damaged house. Neighbors whom she had not met before were helping Alex drape plastic over her roof.

"I have to go," Lieutenant Plate said. "I'm needed elsewhere."

"What can we expect next?"

"It will be at least three to seven days before they get electricity restored and the flooding is just starting."

Jacqueline stood silently as he got into his car and drove off.

Lennon came over to her and took her arm.

"Let's go see what we can do about your broken window while the men waterproof the roof," said Lennon "I had four windows shattered by flying limbs we lost our good pine in the front yard. Uprooted. Darn it. But thank goodness, that was all."

"Greg broke my window. Not the storm."

"Poor, Jean. Poor, Leigh," Lennon said.

The Carston house and the Carter house, side-by-side were completely undamaged.

"Have you seen my cat?"

"I took her to my house," said Lennon. "The girls are playing with her. She's okay and I want you both to stay with us until your house can be repaired. I took in the Carston kitten as well, so Bandit has a companion. Both felines escaped without a mark from the storm. A few scratches may be the result of their developing relationship."

"That sounds wonderful," Jacqueline said gratefully. "We both accept."

A Business Deal

By Deborah DR Kralich

Stars in the purple velvet sky blazed brightly in my eyes as I gulped the Scotch. I was in a part of Paris not visited by members of my family in over 200 years.

Servants at my family's dual estates, responsible for me, each believed I was in the care of coworkers.

Yet arriving at this sidewalk café had been as easy as stepping beyond a gate and hiring a cab.

"First drink, Mademoiselle?" inquired a fatherly looking old waiter. Before I could nod, he continued, "The first is always the hardest. It is better to take it nice and slow."

"Yes. Thank you. I will."

My own voice sounded raspy to my ears.

"What is such a pretty young thing doing all alone in such a deserted corner of Paris? You dress in finery. There is danger here. Those revolution crazies are always looking for opportunities to murder aristocrats." His words were graphic but his tone was busybody light.

"I- I'm waiting for someone," I said, in an obvious attempt to get rid of him.

I cared nothing for revolutions. I had merely used my dance instructor as a means of communication. I knew he sympathized, so would be willing to put me in touch with who I needed. And he had. I glanced at the street as the waiter chatted. Deserted. Good. I wanted no one to notice me.

I pulled my cloak forward about my head.

"Ah." The waiter smiled. "A young man."

"My brother," I lied. "Would you leave me, please?"

By this time I was literally shaking. I saw policeman coming around every corner.

Detectives at every table.

The waiter lingered briefly. Then went to a corner.

I took his advice and sipped slowly. Gradually my fear subsided and glowing warmth took its place. I had come to do what I had to do and I could not back out now.

"Mademoiselle Benet?" I looked, not into the placid face of the waiter, but into the darkly handsome, yet foreboding face of my 'brother'. He was speaking my name with skepticism.

His coal black eyes swept over me as a cat eyes prey. I jumped, violently spilling the rest of my drink all over the flat roundtable.

"I'm terribly sorry. I didn't mean to frighten you. I was looking for a Mademoiselle Benet." He showed gleaming white teeth under a shiny mustache.

"I am Mademoiselle Benet," I said, rising. "Perhaps we should get another table?"

"Yes indeed. The one near the door would be appropriate. Would you like another?"

"No." I stared at his diamond rings and silky black garments. He didn't seem real. He appeared the perfect gentleman, yet I, knowing the truth, suppressed a strong desire to flee.

"Shall we get down to business?" I spoke as lightly as I could manage, still sounding unreal. Surely this was all a dream.

"Yes." He showed his teeth again. "You want to engage my services. What do you desire me to do for you?"

I wished I had taken that other drink. A few minutes elapsed before I could reply.

"I want you to kill someone."

There, I had said it. Burying my head in my hands, I felt sick.

My companion ordered a drink. The waiter regarded us with mock severity for a moment, served the liquor, then retreated again.

"Murder," my companion said, after I had recovered, "is a very serious business. A nasty business."

"I will pay you well. I'm aware of the price."

"Then you know it is high." He spoke with a deathly calm assurance of a professional dealing with an amateur.

"I'm a wealthy woman."

"But how do I know this?"

I took a deep breath. "General Philippe Benet is my father."

"The distinguished general! The hero of our great battle in our last foolish war fought for that foreign Austrian wench. How I hate her loathsome name- Marie Antoinette."

In an instant his charm had melted into vile.

I straightened my spine. I was fond of my kind.

"Forgive me, but I believe my astonishment is understandable. You look so pale, so young not like the 'golden haired social belle' as the newspapers call you."

"I'm old enough to have contacted the most famous, most clever murderer in Paris."

He smiled a little, bowing his head stiffly in the customary way of acknowledging complements. "Still, you're so young. Have you access to your family's wealth?"

I took another deep breath, and reached into my bosom, extracting a small pouch.

His eyes widened. I could see his pulse racing with excitement. He peeked inside.

His outward manner gave no sign of change.

He was good.

"I see. Very well, who would you like disposed of?"

"Madame Cardot."

"Mademoiselle! Do you not know that Madame Cardot is a close friend of the King?"

"Not the elder Madame. Her daughter-in-law, Closine Cardot."

"Still! Such prominent people!"

"Prominent people die easily as peasants," I said bitterly.

"I am afraid-" He started to rise.

"Double!" I cried with desperation. "Take it now. Double, all in gold."

He opened the pouch. Then closed it. He sat back down

"You want her dead badly. She's of the aristocracy. So I understand. But she's not important enough to be worth this much. Our cause will triumph without-"

"I care nothing for any cause." I rose stiffly. "Her husband is my lover. She prevents our marriage."

He drew a sharp breath and stared at me.

"I see. But did I not read that Mademoiselle Benet was to marry the Duke of Seline? The man most trusted by the people and the aristocracy. The one who bridges their gap. That is a ruse? A blind?"

"Yes. He does not care for women." I paused, wondering. Would my companion believe that lie? And what stain would it place on the Duke's character? What consequences would ensue?

I didn't care.

Searching my companion's face with my eyes, with my fingers I gave the pouch a little nudge towards him.

"Half again more when it is done. All in gold. Gold is hard to come by these days."

What did I care what the peasants did with scandal? They were no real threat to us.

His hand poised over the pouch momentarily. Then pounced over it, his fingers covering it like a spider.

"All aristocracy is heavily guarded these days. It is almost impossible to find them outside the palace walls."

"Her nephew is being baptized Sunday. At a small country church. Out of fear, the event has been kept secret and dress will be plain. Your target and-"

I broke off. I couldn't bear to say 'and her husband'-

My companion stared, eyebrows raised.

I swallowed and continued. "And my lover-"

Not actually true yet, but soon!

"Will be godparents." I concluded by handing him a paper with the event details.

"How do you have this information? It is accurate?"

"Our families are close. We'll all be there. Also other

aristocratic personages. Injure no one else. You'll be able to get your target alone without difficulty. She'll slip out the side door sporadically to indulge in tobacco. She'll be the only lady who does this abomination. Do not harm anyone else. Kill only her."

"I understand."

He rose again.

"Aren't you going to count it?" I stood up also.

"No," he said. "You trust me to do the job. I trust you as well, Mademoiselle."

He bowed slightly, then stepped to the corner where the server lounged.

As he paid the bill, they dickered. I paid scant attention even as their insults became louder.

"…savage!…"

"…coward!…"

"…butcher!.."

"…blasphemer!…"

Their petty argument filled me with contempt. I pulled the hood of my cloak closer to my cheeks, blocking out their words.

It would not do for either to know that I had brown hair, not blonde. That I was not the famed Mademoiselle Benet of the society pages but the other Mademoiselle Benet, who, at 14, was too young for formal balls, but not too young to desire a dashing cavalier lieutenant.

A beautiful man, so handsome and irresistible he was fished from the bourgeois by Closine Cardot to be her consort. A heartthrob to die for, who had heretofore paid me only frivolous flirtation, sending windblown kisses.

A practical man who, after suitable mourning for his first wife, wouldn't resist further enhancing his career by taking his famed commander's daughter as his second.

I was sure.

Voices escalated, penetrating. I refocused.

"And the devil himself will condemn you in hell!" the waiter yelled, waiving his arms as my companion turned his back.

Apparently the waiter had been the loser in the bill dispute.

My companion returned. He appeared satisfied.

We faced each other. He nodded, bowing again.

"Mademoiselle," he said. "Au revoir."

He kissed my hand.

Then he walked slowly away down the red cobblestone street. I stood watching him until his dark shadow blended into the starlit night.

Lucretia: A Ghost from the Past

by Deborah DR Kralich

There was no mistake. It was definitely her. Same thin brown-gray hair. Dry colorless eyes. Pale pencil line lips. She was not, he reflected as he had many times, a handsome woman.

She stood oblivious at the corner. An overlarge dark green coat reached down to her knees even though it was only August. The gentle breeze blew her uncombed hair in her face. And with a long thin hand she shoved it back behind her ears.

The light changed.

"Lucretia!" He was shouting, walking towards her.

She heard him, saw him. And for a second, astonishment dominated her features. But only for an instant. Her placid look returned within seconds.

She reached with both hands for his.

"Bobby! Bobby Carlton! After all these years!"

"Hello, Lucretia." His voice echoed finality, inevitability. "It has been a long time. How have you been?"

"Very well, Bobby very well." She nodded. "And you?"

"Oh, fine. Just fine."

Silence. He shifted under her gaze of serenity.

"What brings you to California?" she asked.

"Vacation," he said simply.

She nodded again. "How nice."

"You live here?" His voice was awkward.

"Yes." She paused. "You must forgive me if I'm so suddenly

flustered. One does not expect to meet a ghost of the past on the city streets of Los Angeles."

"No, I suppose not." He was surprised at the unintentional bitterness in his voice. One never gets over those things, he surmised ruefully. Life's major experiences.

"How are they?" she said, praising the inevitable question. "Have you seen them lately?"

"You mean Barney and Carolyn?" He was stalling.

"Ye-es." She inclined her head slightly.

"They are fine. I see them fairly often."

"And Anthony?"

"Well, I hardly ever see him. Last time I did, well, he's growing up to be a fine boy."

She smiled sadly. "And your son? You have him, don't you?"

"No, as a matter of fact I don't."

She arched a thin grey eyebrow in surprise. "But you loved him so much. You should have taken him- I would have taken Anthony if I hadn't- if I could have. Why didn't you take him?"

"It wouldn't have been fair to him." A faint tinge crept into his cheeks.

She looked hard at the pavement. Then at him. "Do you still work there?"

He hesitated.

"Yes."

"Does Barney?"

"Yes."

This upset her. "You work there with Barney?" She moved her cheeks as if the name left a bitter taste in her mouth. "How could you after what they did?" Her monotonous voice gave hint of its capable volume.

He did not reply.

"Don't you want to know when they let me out?" She was taunting him. But her fingers were twitching. It was his turn to stare at the pavement.

She looked at him benevolently. "That was crude. But you really are curious aren't you? Ah well. I won't insist you verbalize it.

It's been two years. Two years ago last month."

"I'm sure you are a better person for it," He said rather weakly.

"Yes," she affirmed. "Yes. I am completely over it. I have a pride and self-respect I never had before."

"I can see that." He paused, remembering Lucretia and Barney, Carolyn and himself. How many times had they socialized formerly and in formally? How many parties? How many Saturdays at the beach with the kids? Carolyn was always her radiant best at the beach- tall, beautiful suntanned, with her titian hair glittering brilliantly on the sand. Lucretia had looked like a dried prune compared to her. Even without the gray hair, the lines of four years of hell, Lucretia had been homely. Carolyn had completely overwhelmed her. Waiters saw Carolyn first. Doormen were quick to take her hand. She never had a problem getting a cab.

Yet Lucretia never seemed jealous. Indeed she had almost reveled in Carolyn's magnetism. Their's had been a strange friendship.

There was nothing strange about his friendship with Barney though. Two successful man with a string of common interest from golf to set the concerts. He'd known Barney and Lucretia long before Carolyn complicated the picture.

They were so different in appearance but so much alike. Barney was almost six foot six but his thinness and extremely fine brown hair discredited his height. Lucretia was too short. So short in fact, that instead of complementing Barney's type, it made them both resemble freaks. Mutt and Jeff.

Lucretia was an awkward person. She lacked her husband's athletic tendency and his fondness for dance. Carolyn loved to dance. She was excellent at it as she was excellent at everything she did. At first it had seemed only natural that Carolyn and Barney dance together, leaving him in Lucretia to their less than stimulating small talk…

"Bobby, what a blank look you have in your eyes!"

He refocused his eyes on Lucretia and sadly he felt a wave of empathy towards Barney. Barney who never had anything but

Lucretia. And what the hell was that? Barney who walked in stars when Carolyn smiled at him. Well, he had Carolyn now, God help him...

"At the institute we had marvelous therapy sessions," Lucretia was saying, "for those of us who only had personal problems..."

'Personal problem' was hardly an accurate description of Lucretia's neurotic breakdown, he reflected grimly.

Had it been only six years ago?

He had been alone except for the baby. Carolyn had said she was going bowling. He had not seen any cause to doubt her word. Around eight the doorbell had begun to ring persistently. He had jumped up immediately in annoyance. The bell would wake the baby and Carolyn wasn't there to comfort him.

Lucretia had burst in screaming like a mad woman. At first he had feared something had happened to Barney or Anthony, their three-year-old. But as Lucretia had raged on, he had begun to grasp what she was saying. An indescribable emotion- not hate or sorrow- but a repulsive frightening anger mixed with a nauseating feeling in the pit of his stomach had taken hold of him.

He cursed first Barney, then Carolyn, then Lucretia who had cowered in the corner, crying. To climax his tirade, he had hurled a vase at the oil painting of Carolyn hanging over the couch. But the vase completely missed the painting and smashed to bits, along with a lamp in its path, on the bare wall.

The baby had begun to scream and Lucretia had numbly went into the nursery to quiet it. While she was gone he had read the proof. Letters, notes, all carefully kept by the lovesick Barney. Then he had seen Lucretia home. And he had returned to wait for the return of his wife.

"You simply got to understand," she had said in her soft lilting voice.

"A whore!" he had raged deliriously. "My wife. The mother of my son! You bitch!"

"Bobby! Don't!" she had pleaded.

"The mother of my son!"

He had stopped then, realizing he could have revenge easily.

"You won't have him." He had spoken calmly but with venom. "You won't have my son."

"What?" Carolyn's eyes had been beautiful in fright.

"I repeat, you get your divorce but you give him up!"

"No," she had begged, crying now. "I know, Bobby! I know I hurt you but I don't deserve to lose my son."

"What was that, Bobby?" Lucretia was peering up at him expectantly. "I didn't quite catch it."

"Oh, nothing, Lucretia. Just thinking."

"I understand, Bobby. It's no crime to remember. I thought about Barney a lot, too. Before," she smiled.

Damn her! How dare she be so smug! Who was she to insinuate his private thoughts were of Carolyn? Even if they were. He smiled grimly. She had not been so very complacent when they carted her off to the nut house. Barney, her only adult relative had made sure she was shipped to faraway California. In an asylum a thousand miles away she could be conveniently forgotten.

But he couldn't do the same with Carolyn.

Now that Lucretia was out she was the model of stability. The cured patient. Did she really think four years of therapy wiped out 15 years of marriage?

One good thing about him and Carolyn. They had only been married three years.

Lucretia was harping on and on about Carolyn.

He began to have pleasant thoughts of murdering Lucretia in various ways.

Strangling. Smothering. Poison.

He grinned.

"Does that so amuse you, Bobby?"

"Huh. Oh. Uh."

Lucretia smiled with satisfaction. "I'm so glad you're doing well. And it's such a pleasure to see you. But you must forgive my asking. How did you ever do it alone?"

"Do what?"

"You know, recover from Carolyn." A drop of venom slid into Lucretia's smile. "I know at first, like me, you were terribly crushed."

Recover from Carolyn. As though she were a fatal disease!

"Yes, you're right, I was," he admitted, not without sincerity. "I hadn't the slightest idea anything was going on between them. But it didn't take long to get over it as far as loving Carolyn was concerned."

"But you adored Carolyn!"

"Did I?" he asked sarcastically. "Maybe so. But I don't recall adoring her now."

"You did," Lucretia said firmly. "YOU followed her around like a little puppy."

"But I did not love Carolyn. I loved what she represented. Elegance. Sophistication. Beauty."

"Nonsense," Lucretia said, neither believing nor understanding him.

"It was a make-believe world Lucretia," he said, almost urgently. "None of us, especially Carolyn, were real."

"When Barney left me the pain was very real."

"But was it the pain of losing Barney or the pain of losing your lifestyle? You had a husband who came home every night and went to bed after the 10 o'clock news. During the day you kept house. What variation there was consisted of eating out or some such family excursion. Usually with us. Suddenly your routine was shattered and you were lost."

"You forget Anthony." She looked suddenly pitiful. "You forget my son. My former son."

"He still is your son. He remembers you."

"He was only seven," she said morosely. "He couldn't have understood. He must believe I left him. Carolyn's his mother now."

He did not say anything. He knew she was right. Anthony was 13 years old. Carolyn had mothered him since second grade. Now he was in junior high.

"She got everything," she cried furiously. "She got my son, my husband, and her son. Two children."

"Three." The word slipped out before he could catch it? Or did it?

Lucretia gasped. "What?"

"Carolyn and Barney have a two-year-old daughter," he said flatly.

Lucretia turned away and he could see she was crying now.

"Why should they have everything and you and I have nothing?"

She turned back to him sobbing, unable to speak for a moment.

"I have something," he said quietly. "You asked me how I got over her. Well, I found someone else. A woman. A real woman. Something Carolyn never was."

Lucretia stared at him, amazed.

"I'd known her for about two years. A friend of a friend. Approximately 2 months after Carolyn left me I accidentally ran into her on the bus. We started dating. Married four months later." He smiled proudly.

"Who?" Lucretia barely managed to keep from choking on the word.

"Sandy McIntyre."

Lucretia shook her head, apparently too stunned to even cry now. Life was passing her by.

"You love her?"

"Of course."

"Children?"

He shifted. "No, she doesn't want children."

"She didn't want your son," Lucretia accused, maliciously. "That's why you don't have custody."

"I didn't say that," he flushed.

"But it's true."

"Yes, it's true," he sighed, exasperated.

"How could you choose a woman over your son?" She glowered at him wildly.

"Hell! There's nothing wrong with it," he practically yelled, causing heads to turn. Quieting down, he added, "a child belongs with its mother. I have him two months a year, every weekend plus most holidays. My wife and I both work. It would not be feasible for us to have him full time. And it wouldn't be fair to my wife to thrust a child upon her that she didn't want. He's happy with Carolyn. He likes Barney. And he knows I'm his father."

He stopped out of breath and excuses.

"I'm sorry it turned out this way for you, Bobby." Lucretia disapproved with a frown. "I had hopes for you."

"Who in hell are you to judge me?" He was outraged. "What do you mean hopes?"

Lucretia explained haltingly. "I'd always thought that we might, well, get together. I mean just to show them."

"Lucretia! That would be madness. Spite." He felt repulsed, offended by the suggestion.

She cringed, offended. "You don't think I'm attractive."

"Now it's not that, Lucretia," he sighed. "But to ru-complicate our lives because of spite would have been crazy."

"It's too late anyway. You are married."

"Yes," he said, softening somewhat. "I'm married to a wonderful girl. You should find someone, too. The past is a finished episode."

"I have a gentleman friend," she said, brightly. "A doctor, in fact."

"That's great!" he said, falsely cheerful.

She frowned thoughtfully. "Will you tell Barney?"

"Not if you don't want me to."

"But I do!" She nodded firmly. "Definitely! I want him to know!"

"I will tell him then." He shifted his weight.

"We're getting married." She clapped her hands. "And we're going to have lots and lots of children!"

For the first time he wondered. Having Anthony had almost killed Lucretia. It was a cesarean section during which she had been sterilized. Perhaps she meant by adoption.

"His name is Everett Hunter. We have set the date for September 20." Lucretia applauded.

"Wonderful, Lucretia. I'm so happy for you."

She smiled contentedly. "We're very happy."

He looked at his watch. "You're not on your lunch hour?"

"No." She looked past him. "Everett doesn't want a working wife."

Neither had Barney.

He looked at her closely. "Sandy wants to work."

"And you don't want her to?"

"I don't mind. After she graduates, but right now it would be too hard on her."

"Graduates! How old is she?"

"Twenty-four."

"Bobby Carlton! You married a child!"

"Not really." He was defending his life to Lucretia again. "There's only seven years between us."

She regarded him indulgently. "You'll get over that infatuation. There can be no one for you except Carolyn, like there can be no one for me except Barney."

He stared at her in astonished fascination.

"Barney will realize this one day and he will want me back." A strange gleam misted her eyes and she pressed the tips of her fingers together. "I won't be there, though. He will want me and I will be gone." She smiled triumphantly, as if what she had described had already taken place.

He blinked. "But what about- ?"

She placed a thin finger to his lips. "Now don't say anything, Bobby. I know how you feel. As I said before it is eerie to meet the past on the modern streets of Los Angeles."

She reached up and kissed him lightly on the cheek. Then she walked quietly yet briskly in the opposite direction from which she had come.

A few feet away from him she turned and called, "Bobby, goodbye. We shall meet again presently."

He stood transfixed, watching her as she reached the corner and waited once more.

The light changed.

Suddenly he was aware of the crowd of bustling pedestrians all around him. They had seemed to disappear as he chatted with Lucretia but now he realized they were a mass of humanity, streaming

60

and flowing in opposite directions, narrowly missing each other.

"Bobby! Bobby! What's the matter with you? You look like you've seen a ghost."

"I have," he said dimly.

"Bobby!" Sandy shook his arm, her long blonde hair shivering impatiently on her shoulders.

No longer entranced, he looked at her with amusement. "You see that woman in the long coat," he said, pointing. "Lucretia Jamison."

"No! You're kidding! She looks like a mouse!"

"You have amazing perception."

"That's really her?"

"Sure is."

Sandy stared.

"She hasn't changed much either," he added.

"How about that! We have got a plane to catch, Robert! In two hours!" she persisted, Lucretia forgotten.

His desire for her intensified. More than he had ever craved any other woman.

"Oh, that's awful." Sandy was scrutinizing a bright red pantsuit in a store window.

Glancing almost reflexively he saw the store name: Everett Hunter Clothing, Incorporated.

With a sharp breath he pivoted, but Lucretia was gone, blending like always into the crowd, out of his life.

Goodbye to Anna Maria

By Deborah DR Kralich

The key did not fit the door.

I shoved it all the way in the hole but the lock wouldn't turn. I thought that Anna Maria must have changed the locks on the house. Then she had forgotten to mention it in her letters. I forced the lock and shoved the door open.

The hallway was dark. It wasn't like Anna Maria to go about the house all shut up. She was a breezy gal, my wife. I grinned as I remembered her earthiness. Obviously she wasn't home although I wrote I was arriving today.

The dear girl had probably dashed out at the last minute for a forgotten but essential food article, hoping against hope she could get back before I arrived. Or for a gift. I was sure she would give me a nice gift. And throw a little party. Nothing fancy, of course.

After all, I had only fought in the war and sustained a minor head wound, not been a hero really, despite what the newspaper said. Just done my duty. No, I only wanted a small welcome home party, a few old friends and dear plump Anna Maria to squeeze while we danced.

The hallway carpet was cushier than I had remembered. I went into the living room. Pale sunlight forced its way switched on the light. My eyes were hit by a blaze of yellow. As in a dream where all objects are the same color, every fixture in this room was a shade of yellow. Long chalky yellow curtains, plush dull sheen yellow couch, thick dirty yellow carpet, pale yellow wall paint. In the middle a sparkling bar that appeared to have been lifted wholly out of a Vegas hotel. The shiny bar was brown wood but it was polished so that it reflected golden rays. All of that yellow would be so beautiful to people who loved yellow.

I've never cared for yellow much.

I had warned myself that Anna Maria would probably make a few changes while I was gone but nothing like this had ever crossed my mind. Anna Maria's tastes certainly had altered. I wasn't prepared for all this. Good heavens, where had she gotten the money to buy this kind of stuff? We must be in debt to our eyeballs.

It dawned on me that Anna Maria was trying to keep up with the neighbors. The neighbors, judging from the surrounding houses, far from having lapsed downward, instead had risen to upper class.

I admit my memories of the house were vague due to my war experiences eclipsing everything else but I knew the last time I saw her the house had been much smaller and not nearly as high class.

She had added square footage as well as redecorated. No wonder she had feared she could not afford to keep it without me. The property taxes must have doubled.

The couch was positioned adjacent to the bar so that it sat in the middle of the room. I walked behind it to peek through the curtains. The sun almost blinded me, making the artificial indoor light dimmer.

A swimming pool had been added. I could see the reflection of sun rays off the water.

A bust on the end table distracted me. It was cheap junk trying to be art. I had an irresponsible impulse to smash it against the patio doors. The silence in the room was disquieting after the constant sounds of battle. The insulting cheap art statue would shatter with a good deafening crash.

I restrained the desire but decided to tell Anna Maria that it had to go. But no matter the decoration, at last I was home. The memory of what I had been through would undoubtedly stay with me forever.

I reached into my breast pocket and drew out the folded newspaper clipping. The last link with my days as a soldier. It was just luck that I came upon the newspaper when I caught a ride on an

18-wheeler. The story was draped across the trucker's passenger seat. He kindly let me cut the page which referred to me without asking why. I debated whether or not to destroy it as I unfolded it and read it again for the hundredth time.

The story was in grave error factually but it did give a generous description of me:

> *Col. Lamb Returns Home to Wife Last Time*
> *Houston, TX- Colonel Dennis Lamb, 32, winner of the Congressional Medal of Honor, killed in service of his country, comes home, Wednesday, to be buried in the Texas metropolis. Lamb, veteran of numerous wartime and a valued member of the elite Army Corps of Engineers, perished during a controlled explosion mishap an army spokesman said. Lamb was struck in the head by falling debris, taken to a hospital where he was sedated in hopes of limiting the effects but he died. The serviceman is survived by a loving wife, Anna Maria, a former resident of Kansas City before her marriage to the Texas soldier- cont p.4*

Of course, I was upset when they reported me dead.

I called the newspaper from a pay phone and gave them hell. They told me I was crazy.

I contacted the army to make sure they got the facts straight. But the service doesn't make mistakes, only newspapers, they said. Due to my being very much alive, I told them to call off the memorial service. Just give me a bus ticket home. But they would not spring for that, cheapskates, they hung up on me. Out of change, I had to hitchhike. That was not a problem. Anna Maria and I were veteran hitchhikers in our early youth. Hiked all over the US until we settled down in the home pictured next to my story. I was a little disconcerted they put my address under the picture and there was a for sale sign on it. But the sign had a black line through it so I knew if Anna Maria had toyed with the idea of selling it she had changed her mind. Having a home of our own had been a dear dream of ours.

She might have thought if I did not return from the war she could not afford to keep it. Then realized I was coming back and she need not worry.

So here I was.

Suddenly exhaustion attacked me and I barely managed to switch off the light before falling on the couch. I was flushed with warmth. Home from the war at last, stretching out on my own couch, even if it wasn't exactly the same couch I had left going off to war, gave me a good feeling. I closed my eyes.

It been a long tiring journey.

I was like a drunk man when I awoke. I stumbled off the couch. On my hands and knees between it and the coffee table, my fingers groped and dug through the dark glowing carpet as though searching for a lost pearl. I wasn't sure where I was. I tried to get up but a strong smell of paint made me dizzy and I could only rise to my knees. A cloud of dirty gray yellow fog covered the room. My eyes had to strain to see. I remembered I was home.

A blonde fashion doll had come to life and she was standing in the door way. A long golden evening gown shimmered and a cloak of chicken feathers shook. In the dim haze I couldn't discern her features. Was it Anna Maria, thirty pounds slimmer and with dyed blond hair?

"Are you a burglar?" Her light and saucy voice did not sound like Anna Maria.

"No," I said, on my knees.

"A leftover from last night?"

"No," I said. I couldn't move.

She came closer, throwing her wrap over her shoulder dramatically. Feathers flew.

A bad actress in a B movie.

She perched on the arm of the couch,

"Well, then, stranger, just who the hell are you and why are you kneeling down between my couch and my coffee table?"

"Anna Maria?" I still couldn't make out her face clearly.

"Is Anna Maria under the couch?" Her tone suggested I was

amusing her. The smell of liquor replaced the smell of paint.

"Do you live here?" My fist hit the coffee table involuntarily.

"Last time I noticed," she said. "Hey, did you break the lock on my door?"

"Then you are Anna Maria," I said, reaching for her. "It's me. It's Dennis. I'm home."

She rose, backing away,

"When did you dye your hair blond? Aren't you glad to see me? You haven't taken up with, oh, some other man have you?" I walked forward on my knees, my arms stretching out to her.

"Listen," she said, very fast and with a small laugh. "If you're a Moslem and you needed some place to stop and pray to Mecca when the time came, it's perfectly okay with me. That you broke in. See?"

She switched on the light and the fog vanished. No longer dizzy but still shaky, I rose.

"If you need some food. Some in the dining room. You look hungry. Money, I got a little cash here."

She kept on talking but I tuned her voice out to study her face. Her hair did not appear dyed. It was almost white but a tinge of yellow kept it from being platinum. It shown so that it almost appeared synthetic. Her nose was Anna-Maria.

But the mouth- if it were just a little bit more to the left.

Maybe it was the brand of lipstick she was using now. The forehead was too high but I supposed the dye had caused the hairline to recede and the eyes, oh, but no! The green eyes were not Anna Maria! What could be done to those eyes to make her Anna Maria again? Contact lenses to change shape and color? Eye make-up? Glasses? Sunglasses? My brain fitted all of them on her.

Nothing could make up for such a difference in those green eyes.

"Why have you changed so much, Anna Maria?" I interrupted her chatter.

"Andrena," she said.

"What?" I moved towards her.

"Andrena. My name's Andrena. But, hey, if you want to call

me Anna Maria, hey, it's OK."

"And you live here? How long have you lived here?"

"How long, oh, gee, don't know. I can't think, several years." She licked her lips and waved her fingers in the air.

"Did you buy the house from Anna Maria?"

"Uh, no, I, uh, bought it from an old man, or was it an old woman, no I'm sure it was an old man- uh, do you mind if I get a drink? Want one?"

"No, thank you. But go right ahead. You say you are not Anna Maria?"

"No." She poured a Scotch. "Don't know her I'm afraid. Is she your girl?"

"My wife," I said. I noticed the glass shook a little. "Hey, don't be scared. I'm not a burglar or rapist or Moslem or anything. I'm just home from the war. Actually I got out a few days ago but it took me a while to get here."

"Home from the what?" She poured another.

"War."

"Home from the- war?"

"Yeah, just got out of the uniform last Monday. And this is where my wife lives- or lived. You must have bought the house from her. Now think. Wasn't the old man just the real-estate agent?"

"Home from the war." She took a long drink.

"Right. You know. The war."

"Gee." She sat down on the couch, "I've been missing 'World News Tonight' too much lately. I didn't even know there was a war going on."

I laughed. The booze was obviously getting to her. Who could forget the war?

"I really." She hiccuped. "Didn't know it. You'd think someone would have told me. What's this one called?"

"I don't want to talk about the war," I said. "I just want to find my wife. I was on the front lines a long time so my contact with her was erratic. The letter she must have wrote about moving must have not got through. I know things at the homefront have frequently been as hectic as things at the battlefield so I understand her not writing too much."

"I really didn't know."

"Can you remember the name of the real estate agent?"

I was getting a little impatient. Darkness was spreading over the city and I needed to get to Anna Maria tonight.

"I told you there wasn't one."

I paced, trying to control my temper. "The old man," I said, gritting my teeth.

"That's who I bought the house from."

"No. You bought it from Anna Maria Lamb, a young, brown headed, plumpish girl. Olive complexion. My wife."

"I never- hick- knew her."

I grabbed the cheapest art statue I could find and I smashed it on the floor.

"Dammit, think!"

"No," she said, cowering on the couch, holding her whiskey glass up as a shield. "No, I'm sure. That was, um, valuable."

I grabbed an ash tray and nervously aimed it at the patio doors. "I'll ask one more time."

She jumped off the sofa and grabbed hold of me around the waist in defense of her patio doors.

"Oh, please, Dennis, not my patio doors!"

The sound of my name was so foreign that I froze.

Had I told her my name?

Once, maybe, but how had she caught it so quickly if she were not Anna Maria?

I jerked away from her and threw the ashtray on the sofa.

"If you've forgotten where you live. If you've got no place to go, well, you can stay here for the night," said Andrena, as she smoothed her hair.

"I've waited so long for Anna Maria."

"I'll call my lawyer tomorrow. He'll know who I bought the house from."

"Can't you call him now?" I said, almost pleading. "It's not late."

"I'll call but the results are iffy. I'll have rivals for his attention." She considered, licking the tips of her fingers. "After midnight maybe we could spend some time together. Maybe go for a swim, OK?"

"OK."

She left the room to make the call. I jerked open the curtain and stared through the patio doors and the pool water glistening in soft moonlight.

"What did your lawyer say?" I asked when she returned.

She had a strange look on her face. "He asserts that I'm right." She went to the bar and poured more whiskey. "There isn't any war going on."

"No war? No damn war?" I took her by the shoulders and pulled her around to face me. The whiskey sloshed out of the bottle. Some of it landed on my cheek. "You're telling me I'm lying? I spent months and months fighting on the front lines and you're telling me there is no damn war?"

"You're hurting me." She batted her eyes hard and mascara fell on her cheeks.

I let go of her shoulders.

"All right, I'm not saying I don't believe you. Calm down. Just tell me- what's the name of this war?"

"Do you want its damn address and phone number too?" I curled my lip in a snarl. "Going to invite it to a party?"

She sighed deeply and I felt like a bratty kid.

"You say you just got back?" I could tell she was trying to be open minded.

"Yes." I attempted to lower my voice.

"You were fighting in this war two weeks ago?"

"A week ago."

"The last war we had was in Vietnam," she said.

"Were you in Vietnam?"

"Yes, yes I was there. Listen, it's boring talking about it."

"Vietnam was years ago."

"The one after that, too. The one going on right now. There's always a war going on," I said. I thought I was exhibiting amazing patience.

"There was one before that- Korea, but you're not old enough."

"Hell, it's all too damn confusing which war was when where-"

"Perhaps you were a mercenary." She spoke as though this were a brilliant revelation from above. "Now, let's see. Afghanistan? El Salvador? Lebanon!"

"No, dammit no! I was in an American war. I said it was a real war. Look at this-" I lowered my head and pushed back enough hair to reveal the inch thick of freshly gathered skin crisscrossing my scalp. "Does that look like an American war scar to you? Could it be anything else?"

Andrena gently ran her slender long nailed fingers over the scar. The pink finger tips caressed then the whole of my face, smoothing down crumpled hair gliding over the unblemished skin on my forehead.

"No, it couldn't be anything else," she conceded. That issue was settled.

"You were in a war." Andrena danced with gliding movements in a circle in front of me. "In the American army. And you just got home from active duty- the fighting."

"Yes." I leaned against the bar watching the golden gown shine.

Andrena poured more whiskey, wet her lips, then stared into the glass. Shrugging, she sat down on the couch. As she crossed them, her tan velvet legs peeked out from the slit in the dress. She picked up a newspaper.

"It doesn't matter where," I said. "What about that swim?"

She dropped the paper.

"Although it's about fifty degrees outside," I said.

She turned off the light.

"I've known Novembers much warmer than this. Some in the seventies," I said.

She took off her gown and her shoes.

"Is the pool heated? Why do you keep it full even in the winter? We'll probably catch pneumonia."

She took off her slip, her hose.

"Won't the neighbors see?" I asked.

She too off her bra, her panties, everything...

We were naked in the pool. In the pale moonlight I often lost sight of her. She sent the water over my head in waves that were like those in the ocean. She was a sea goddess who could compel the water to do her bidding. I stood with my back to the pool wall and she and the water came at me again and again. The water was warm and dark. She was dark, too, except for her glittering hair.

I reached for her in the water. I wanted to caress her in the water. But she always sent the water at me, plastering me against the wall, laughing as the water rose above my head filling my eyes, ears and nose with chlorine, then dropping back down so the wind could chill my face. I wanted desperately to feel her skin in the water but all I could grasp was water.

At last she dove under and I went after her, trying in vain to catch her feet but they kicked too much water in my face. She climbed out and ran across the cement to the patio doors. I was shaking by the time I got into the living room. She was already half-way up the stairs. Somewhere in the house a clock I'd never heard before began chiming.

"Hey," I shouted. "What did we do out there? Did we make love in the water?"

"No," she said. "You made love to the water."

And her laughter, blending with the chimes, bubbled like wispy white foam in the sea.

***

"Mr. Lamb," said the lawyer as he mixed drinks at the bar. "All deed and title history of this house show that there was never an owner by the name of Dennis Lamb. Here, Andrena, my dear." He handed her a drink.

I came forward on the couch until I was merely squatting on its edge. "I was the owner of this house before I went to war."

"Mr. Lamb." The lawyer smiled a toothpaste commercial smile. "You never owned this house."

"Yes, he did," said Andrena, blinking as the bright sunlight from the patio doors reflected off her glass. "He owned this house."

"You're only hurting yourself, Andrena," said Marvin. "All the time, that's all you ever do."

"That's my business, Marvin."

Marvin shifted. "So you were in the war, Mr. Lamb?"

"That's right, I don't like to talk about it."

"The Vietnam war took a terrible toll on this country's morale and the minds and bodies of her men. Wouldn't you agree, Mr. Lamb?"

"I've never really thought about it."

"Dammit, Marvin," said Andrena. "Stop cross examining my guest."

"Andrena, don't you realize this man's just another moocher. Just another stray you've picked up. Just like the others, he will cost you money." He turned to me. "Just because Andrena was born independently wealthy and slightly flighty, people think they can get away with taking advantage of her generous nature."

"Flighty? Damn you, Marvin. Right to hell!"

"In the end, Andrena knows who looks after her interests." Marvin got all red and puffy in the face. "Andrena knows who cares about her."

"Get out, Marvin. Go on and leave. I don't like you right now."

"Yes, Marvin." I felt like a host at a party. "Go on and leave. Andrena and I will wash the glasses without you."

"Dennis and I can manage on our own now. And I don't care how much money he costs. I can cover the bill."

"Andrena, just please listen to this man. Consider all the stories he's told you about nonexistent wars. How do you explain, huh? He's nuts. Nuts."

"Battle fatigue," said Andrena. She picked up a brush from the coffee table and began brushing her hair.

"What?" Marvin jumped off the barstool.

"In my estimated opinion he has battle fatigue."

Andrena tugged at a tangle.

"When you get tired of this freeloader call me," said Marvin, jerking his coat on. "Call me and I'll get rid of him for you just like I got rid of all the rest."

Marvin left in a huff.

Andrena was pouting as she started up the stairs. She turned and looked down at me.

"I didn't mean to cause trouble for you with your boyfriend."

"HIM? My boyfriend? Don't you give me any credit for any sense? Any taste?" She glowered.

"Sorry. No offense, OK?"

"I want you to do a favor for me," she said, her face softening.

"Anything within reason, of course."

"I have a tangle in my hair I can't get out."

Her golden white hair reached almost to her waist and it was like silk against my hands. She was sitting on the corner of her bed with her back to me. It was the first time I had been in her room. It was all done in green. It reminded me of a bright and soft green garden that I had once seen as a child.

But that garden had lacked flowers as beautiful as Andrena.

"Ouch, dummy, that's my head, not a mop."

"How can I get it out without pulling?"

"Grab the hair and hold it high about the tangle while you brush."

As I bent over and brushed out the tangle, her head touched my cheek.

"You're such a fascinating man, Dennis. So mysterious. I like fascinating and mysterious men."

"What do you do, Andrena?"

"I do lots of good things."

"I mean profession." Seductress, most likely.

She stretched back on the bed. "Actress."

"Work often?"

She held out her arms. "Not in three years. Come to me." She unbuttoned her dress and slipped her panties to her feet with a minimum of movement.

I was going to have her on top of the spread. She didn't even bother to push back the cover. I didn't like that. I stared down at her. Her panties binding her feet. Her purple cotton dress spread open resting to either side of her body. Then the gleam flared in her eyes. The Anna Maria gleam. She was Anna Maria! I fell back from her, nauseated in the core of my belly.

"Anna Maria, Anna Maria, why have you changed so much?"

Andrena sat up with a jump, hugging her dress to cover her nakedness.

"Anna Maria, Anna Maria, Anna Maria," I said over and over. "Anna Maria, Anna Maria..."

"Anna Maria! There is no Anna Maria," cried Andrena, with fury and hurt in her eyes. "Anna Maria never was. Just like the war doesn't exist, Anna Maria doesn't exist!"

I wanted to hit her. I grabbed her dress and tore it. I raised my palm. Her eyes widened in fear, waiting for my blow to strike.

I could not do it.

Instead I fled. Like a coward I turned tail.

"Who are you, Dennis?" she said, as I ran out the door. Her voice was choked. "Who are you?"

It was very cold this night. The wind stung my eyes I tried to focus my mind on Anna Maria. Her features escaped me. I wished there had been a picture of her with the newspaper article. I could only remember that her hair was brown but Andrena's was golden white blond that sparkled against a purple cotton dress. I saw Andrena's eyes. I saw the gleam turn to hurt and fury. I saw her small hands covering her eyes. I saw all that in sequence like a home movie. I saw the movie an infinite number of times for every step I walked.

I checked every car parked along the sides of the streets in the neighborhood. Only the owner of a small red car had neglected to lock a door. I crawled into the back seat, having to fold double to lie down. There I spent the night. I was sure I had spent the night in more crazy and more colder places during the war but, like Anna Maria, their memory escaped me.

The next morning when I got home Andrena was drunk. Barefooted, her hair a knotted mess, she draped, curled like a snake on the couch. "Mime drunk," she said. Her voice was thick.

"What happened to your hair?"

"I washed it," she said. She waved her hands at me with

drunken exaggeration. She tried to run her fingers through the hair but her hand hung in the twisted gnarled mess. "Hee, hee, I guess I forgot to comb it fore it dried. Do you, crazy sir, crazy sir who just came from a war that doesn't exist, do you know why 'm drunk?"

"And your shoes?"

She stuck her lower lip out in a pout. "In the swimming pool, threw them in - spppplash!" She thrust her arm down, breaking a nail on the carpet.

I sat down on the couch, took her shoulders and gently guided this docile angel upright.

"Do you know why 'm drunk?"

"No."

She jerked away so fast that I did not let go of her dress and it ripped.

"Look at me! See me!"

I saw. She tottered before me, hair a grisly fright wig, red eyes, red cheeks, red nose, one breast hung out of the torn gold evening gown, hem wadding on the floor because the lack of shoes made her four inches shorter.

I suppressed a desire to laugh with difficulty.

"Look at me! I'm beautiful! I should be a movie star or a first lady or at least a senator's wife. I'm society m-material. M-my name should be in lights- cause I'm special. But no! I live in a fine house- dress good- look at this dress- but people see Andrena and say 'who the hell cares?' "

I was laughing hysterically by then, beating the couch arm, stomping the floor.

"Dennis, you low down bastard, you laugh."

The hiss in her voice and the tears spilling from her eyes caused me to try to straighten my face. After all I had come back to make amends, I was even prepared to let her live in the house for a while until Anna Maria came back. For a while. Until she got a new place. For as long a while as she needed. For a long, long while. I got up and reached for her but she jumped back, stepping on the dress, ripping it further. I couldn't help but hoot wildly. She and the dress crumpled to the floor in defeat. In a second all the laughter was out of me. Somberly I helped her up. She held the ripped dress out to me as if she expected me to mend it. She grabbed my shoulders to steady herself. My hands were around her waist. I smelled for her liquor breathe but the only detectable odor was her expensive perfume.

"Dennis." She licked her lips.

"Changed to vodka." I was whispering,

"Dennis, aren't you going to take m-me and take me up to the bedroom, then, m-make love to m-me?"

"Don't you remember what happened last time? I almost hurt you." I felt like a father talking to a small shaking child. "Aren't you angry?"

"No, you don't find me 'ttractive?"

"It's not that. You don't remember. You're drunk. I could have hurt you. I don't want to hurt you."

"You don't find me desirable." She ran her index finger across my eyebrow.

"It's not that."

"Then, Dennis!"

In her reddened green eyes I saw my reflection.

Ah, sweet white bed and golden streamers. Sweet smell of skin and sweet taste of salt. Woman, woman, have you not by the grace of God, chose to wrap your red lips around man to frame him with golden curls? Woman have you not chosen the flesh, the bronze skin, rather than the light divinity of the clouds as your habitat. Do you not want it this way?

I and Andrena. Andrena and I. We, together, only our feet cover by the indiscreet sheet.

"I like you better when you're sober," I said.

"Mmmm." She got up and poured a drink from the bottle on the dresser. She brought the whole bottle into bed and drank. "I'm sober now."

And so she was.

"Everything is backwards since the war," I said.

Without warning the most horrible feeling hit. I was choking, paralyzed, my eyes and lungs burning from searing air.

"Andrena, help me. Andrena." I was gasping, I couldn't

breathe.

She wrapped her arms around my shoulders and pressed my head to her bosom. At once I began to feel a healing release from pain. Pain so chronic I had taken it for granted for years, not realizing the depth of the aching until its relief.

"I'm here, Dennis, I'm here. I'll always be, if you want me. Just don't ever leave. Stop searching and don't ever leave me."

"I won't." The atmosphere cooled back down and I lifted my head from her breasts and stared into her smooth green eyes.

"Are you all right? What happened? Are you ill?"

"It was the war. The enemy came back."

"Tell me about the war." She genuinely wanted to know.

I struggled to recall. "We were one time in golden wheat fields. The wheat was so beautiful, ready to harvest. It waved with the wind. So peaceful- back and forth, back and forth. Then the enemy came and it all turned to red and black, I don't remember any more. Let's make love again."

Soon after we fell asleep.

I dreamt I beat Andrena.

I slapped her just hard enough so that her head snapped backwards. Then I grabbed my belt and lashed her. I whipped red and blue stripes across her white breasts, her belly, thighs, legs. She covered her eyes with her hands and cried out loudly each time the belt touched her but she made no move to run or fight back. I was going to kill her for she stood in the way of Anna Maria coming back to me. I gripped my belt, preparing to strangle…

I awoke a sweat. Andrena slept contentedly beside me. My intense relief diminished quickly. It was the middle of the night. The house was being attacked.

Bullets rained, bombs blasted.

Andrena awoke and she screamed. With each blast, a forgotten picture grew sharper and sharper. Anna Maria was trapped, defenseless.

"I've got to get to Anna Maria," I said, pulling my clothes on. "The enemy's attacking."

"No, Dennis, no, don't leave me for Anna Maria. I love you,

Dennis. Don't forsake me, don't go, don't go. I beg you."

Andrena was crying and holding to me but I felt nothing but concern for Anna Maria. I pushed her to the floor and ran downstairs. She stood at the top of the stairs screaming as I unlocked the front door.

"Don't come back, don't come back, you idiot! It's only a storm, only a thunderstorm. Don't come back! You'd leave me for a myth, oh, damn you! Don't come back!"

I flew out the door and a waterfall of rain hit me in the face.

The action was too intense. I failed to find Anna Maria. I found the same unlocked car and took shelter, hoping for a lull in which to try again. Inadvertently I fell asleep.

When the sun shown again as if the storm never happened, I came back home, Andrena was not yet awake. I thought with satisfaction that I had her in the palm of my hand now. She was obviously in love with me.

Although she would have to leave before Anna Maria came home.

Again I felt an odd discomfort when I tried to see Anna Maria.

I pulled the old newspaper clipping out of my pocket. It was my ace in the hole, my vital link with Anna Maria. It proved I was telling the truth. But I must have folded it wrong because I opened it to the other side. Hurriedly I flipped it over. My story was still there. Relieved, I reversed the clipping again. I did not recall the other side.

Mystery Survivor Vanishes from Hospital

Kansas City- The lone survivor of a tornado, which touched down Wednesday and destroyed a passing recreational vehicle on CR43 disappeared from the hospital today. The storm only did minor damage elsewhere but struck the RV head on in the roadway killing a woman inside, at first thought to be the only victim. The man had been found a day later wandering in the remote rural farm area, dazed from a head injury. Estimated to be between 30 and 35 years of age, he was too incoherent to contribute any information about himself or the woman. Hospital personnel had sedated him with the hope he would regain his cognition upon waking and be able to verify his and the dead woman's identities but instead he fled.

Police were frustrated that the man evaded hospital personnel but medical authorities insisted the man had been comatose. Police were skeptical of the hospital's claim the man had not been left alone as they did not report him missing immediately after finding his bed empty. While the body of a woman was recovered from the RV, which caught fire, was burned to the point of being unidentifiable, it was determined the woman died from injuries consistent with those suffered by storm victims. Police say they will continue to seek the man but since no crime was committed their functions were limited. Although the man apparently took clothing, personal items, and a small amount of cash contributed for him, all of which had been stored in the room with him, police declined to designate that action as theft, saying the items legally could be claimed as belonging to him and (cont on p 8)

Interesting. But I could not be concerned with other people's stories just right now. I turned it back to my story and read it again, trying to picture Anna Maria. Trying to remember the war. The picture was oddly distorted in my mind. The clear image of her in her little white apron baking in the kitchen had sustained me throughout the war. Now it had yellowed and faded like a weathered photograph. If I never found Anna Maria (I was surprised at my lack of distress at that thought) then there wouldn't be any reason for Andrena to leave at all.

I was relaxing on the couch when Andrena came in. I had to admire her. She showed no signs whatsoever of having been upset. She was crisply attired, rather as though she were conducting business.

"Back to the old standby," I said as she poured whiskey. I slouched, trying to be nonchalant as I searched her face in vain for any trace of emotion.

"I've decided," she said in an unreadable monotone, "to let you stay."

I smiled.

"There will be certain terms."

"Naturally." I grinned.

"You may stay here and live in my house. You may pass yourself off as my husband, even. If you so desire."

I stopped grinning. She had the air of a grade teacher reading class announcements.

"I'll add your name to my checking accounts and credit cards. I have a bottomless pit of money." She took a deep breath. The most important announcement was forthcoming. "And I will let you call me," she paused as though the next words were almost unbearable. "I will let you call me Anna Maria if you wish."

She waited for the impact of this statement.

I couldn't think of anything to say.

"One other thing," she said, "our relationship will be strictly platonic. No sex." She looked me straight in the eye. I was chilled. "You may seek out other satisfactory company for sex. Just do it discreetly and try not to get any diseases. Understand?"

"You want me to live platonically with a drunken lush who thinks she should be a movie star?"

The words made no dent in her.

"Lush and drunken are synonyms, thus redundant in the same sentence."

"Listen, you can't do this to me."

"You don't understand. I will play Anna Maria for you. You win. I will even change my hair to brown."

Oh that beautiful silvery blond hair! "I didn't mean to insult you. I really am sorry."

I was confused. I didn't feel like a winner.

"I have erased that."

"And making love to me?"

"I was drunk. I plead extenuating circumstances."

"I can still find the real Anna Maria,"

"You can stay here or you can to go to the nut house. Nobody believes your war story."

"You do." I was sure she believed me. I tried to re-experience the horror of the war. It had always come so easily before. I couldn't quite grasp it.

"Yes, I do. But the war's over. You belong here now. "

"You want me to say I'll never touch you?"

"Never."

"Well, I wouldn't, I wouldn't feel anything for you. I wouldn't want you."

"Right."

"Other people believe me." I knew that was a lie. I searched her face again. There was no glean in her eyes. I poured myself a scotch and her another. Then an idea crystallized and I jumped in relief.

"You want me to stay? Just tell me why if you don't feel anything. Just why do you want me here? If you don't feel for me what difference does it make? Aha! I've got you there!"

"What difference could it make?"

"We all have dreams. You have Anna Maria. Well, after you came here I had a dream too. I guess I had one before that I can't remember. But I had you for a time. But you ruined my dream because I wasn't your dream. I wasn't Anna Maria."

She faced me.

"I want you to stay," she said, very slowly, "so I can watch you grow just like me."

I staggered, stunned, confused again. Then she spit on me, without emotion, and not very well, for it landed on my shirt instead of my face. Yet it had the same desired effect.

"I'm going to watch you grow just like me." Her eyes narrowed and I was astonished to see that I had been wrong all that time, her eyes were not green but yellow, lifeless yellow.

"I can leave," I said, although I knew those words were useless.

"No you can't. You've won. You can't walk away from victory,"

I had won. But an empty victory. The wheat field was captured all burnt and black and useless. Destroyed.

I grabbed an unopened bottle of scotch and a glass. I walked behind the couch to the patio doors. I saw the top of her golden white head resting against the top of the sofa. Fresh air came from the patio doors as I opened them. The sun cast a bright yellow through dirty grey clouds. I sat by the swimming pool fully intending to get drunk. But after finishing the whole bottle, I still wasn't drunk. I rose to go back into the house.

I glanced down. At the bottom of the pool were two stained aqua evening shoes. One had landed upright, the toe pointed away from the drain. The other had fallen on its side.

I squatted and rippled the water above them with my fingers, causing the water to become a blurry aqua green. Anna Maria. Anna Maria was a hard dream to let go of. Yet I couldn't remember the picture anymore... she was eating?... no...cooking?... I couldn't find the memory. I had lost all sensation of her. Anna Maria had become as impossible to catch as the little waves I made in the water. I would never hold her.

I knew what serious harm I had done.

I had destroyed Andrena's dream.

But maybe not completely.

I needed to put the green gleam back in those eyes. Maybe it wouldn't be an easy battle to recapture the gleam. But wasn't I a soldier? I would prepare. I would be ready. I would win and her eyes would glow green once more. I would succeed.

Suddenly I even knew how. I would endeavor to return that healing comforting touch. That was the key. That was the secret weapon.

I caressed the bright blue water again.

"Good-bye, Anna Maria, wherever you are. Good-bye, Anna Maria," I said, pitching the bits of newspaper to the little waves. "Good-bye, Anna Maria."

Then I turned towards Andrena.

The Iced Trap

by Deborah DR Kralich

I so often think of home as I stare out the frosted window.

The child sleeps.

My husband reads his worn collection of medical journals over and over again.

And I just stand at the iced window and remember home and how we were before.

And I am terribly afraid.

Twilight is fading and darkness is creeping in.

I turn from the window to pace. There is nothing to do here except an hour of housework each morning. A little cooking each day. The cabin is so small. In the living area a desk stuffed with medicines and other physician's supplies takes up precious space, barely leaving room for a small couch, a chair, and a coffee table. Two coal oil lamps and a fireplace provide our only light.

In the one bedroom the child cries.

At once Gregory jumps up.

"I'll go," he says.

"She's such a nervous child," I say. The words are inadequate. I am inadequate with respect to the child's needs.

It is one more way I fail my husband.

Outside it snows and snows and snows...

The Great Snowstorm of 1978.

Parking on our doorstep like an unwelcome stranger...

"You got her back to sleep," I say when Gregory comes back.

83

"She was frightened," he says.

I walk in front of the fire, clasping my arms in front of me. I am cold. "I don't blame her."

Gregory stands behind me, his hands on my shoulders.

We have been over this many times before. But he knows I am not satisfied. I want to go over it again.

"We are safe here," he says.

"Safe." I close my eyes. Safe is warm sunshine and hot gentle breezes. Hell isn't hot. Hell is cold- cold air that hits the back of your throat like a knife when you breathe.

He hugs me tightly from behind, enveloping my folded arms as if he is desiring to warm me. In response (I must show a response), I tilt my head back against his cheek.

"We have enough food and heating fuel to last," he says. "Even if we're snowed in here for several days."

I turn around in his arms, my face against his shirt, "It's never comfortable here. It's always so cold."

He drops his arms and backs away from me. "We couldn't leave, Anna. State police supervised the evacuation."

"There isn't a chance in a million anyone would notice us."

"It was a chance we couldn't take."

"They may still come to evacuate us. The snow is not so high yet."

"They'd have already come if they were going to. All the highways are probably frozen over by now."

"Then, we're trapped."

"It does not matter if we're trapped. So long as they don't find us. So long as they don't know we're here."

The child cries again and Gregory trudges back to the bedroom.

I edge closer to the fire. I am always cold.

Like a sonic boom within a nightmare comes a loud rapping at the door. It is the police come for us at last to take Gregory away from me, to wrench us apart...

I hear my own screams.

Gregory runs from the bedroom as the rapping continues. He

bounds to the desk and gets a gun. He moves in front of the couch and points the weapon unsteadily at the door.

"Open the door!" he orders. "Then stand behind it. Get out of the way fast."

I only gaze at him.

"Open the door, Anna! Open the door!"

I shade my eyes as if the snow would blind me like the hot white sun back home in Texas.

I no longer visualize continuous movement. I see only in flashes. Rapid projection of still life slides.

I see the gun in Gregory's hand.

I see in swift staccato sequence- the snow falls in, the man falls in, the woman falls in.

I am frozen as the wind whips me. Gregory pulls me away from the open door, the gun still leveled at the couple.

But they notice neither us nor the gun. The man lies flat on his back on our floor, bleeding from his head. The woman protectively holds him, whispering to him. There is tenderness in her manner that transcends the blowing icy bitterness and warmly comforts the man.

My husband evolves from a hunted criminal into a doctor. After a second of indecision, he hands the gun to me as he guides the woman to the chair. With a struggle, I close the door. Then I return the gun to the desk.

Gregory carries the man to the couch. He fights at Gregory, trying to get up. Gregory restrains him until he falls back, losing consciousness.

"What are you doing? What are you doing to him?"

The shivering woman rises unsteadily.

"It's all right," I say as I go to her.

"It's all right. I'm a doctor. I'll take care of him." Gregory speaks with authority.

She almost laughs. "A doctor?"

"Yes, my husband is a doctor. Everything will be all right."

We are all silent a moment as Gregory looks at the man's injury. Then the child begins to cry. Awakened and frightened by the noises, she is standing by the fireplace. Uncertainty shows once again on Gregory's face. Who comes first? The injured man or the child?

He goes to the child. Wordlessly he bends down and she clasps him. He rises with her in his arms.

"Do you want me to take her?" I ask.

"No, check him. I think he just passed out."

Gregory and his child cling to one another.

I feel the man's wrist then I turn to the woman. She tells me her name and gives a brief explanation of what happened to them. She allows me to lead her to the bedroom, agreeing to change into some of my clothes. I leave her alone in the bedroom. I cannot stand to watch her remove her soaked clothes for they are new, the latest style in sportswear. And as soon as she shakily peeled them from her skin and dropped them to the floor I would be prey to an irresistible urge to pick them up and hold them against me in front of a mirror just to see how I would appear in clothes less than two years old.

To avoid such a frivolous action in a time of crisis, I return to the living room.

The child has fallen back to sleep on the chair.

"The woman's changing clothes," I say. "What about the man? We shouldn't try to get warm clothes on him?"

"Just get some blankets to cover him. I don't want him to move at all until I can determine just how bad his head injury is."

"Is he going to survive?" My hope that the man lives is sincere. Nothing would be better for Gregory's self-esteem than to help a patient again.

"There's a good chance." Gregory is full of pensive excitement. "I have so little here to help him with."

"You worked back home many times in limited circumstances."

"So many of those people. All those years. So much work. So much accomplished. And how am I repaid?"

"It's my fault. I know."

"Oh, Anna, it's not your fault. But I know you regret what we did. I can see more and more regret in you every day." Gregory leans against the wall as if he can no longer stand without support. "You miss home too much."

I stare at the snow covered window and think of the bright sun shining on a Texas barn. "I'd follow you anywhere. You know that. Besides it was my inadequacy. I did not give you a child."

And I cannot love the child you have now, I think silently. I cannot be her mother as you are father.

I thought I could. I believed I would naturally grow to love her. But I was so wrong, so dreadfully wrong.

I fail again.

"We have a beautiful child now," says Gregory. "No one could ask for a more beautiful daughter."

No! I want to snarl at him. No! She's not my child. She can't ever be. I hate her for what she has done to you, for the change she has caused in you. God knows I try not to be so unfeeling, so empty. But I have nothing inside my heart for that child.

But I do not say any of this.

"Don't you have any regrets? Don't you ever wish you hadn't?"

An expression of suicidal desperation comes over him so fast that I am alarmed. His skin turns chalky white.

"Every night I live it all over again in my dreams." He pauses. "I don't believe I could ever take another life. But I'm so afraid I will have to kill again to keep my child. I will do it. And then I would go mad." He pauses once more and gazes at the child. "She is my flesh and blood. I must have her with me. I must keep her."

"You'll never have to kill again," I say to comfort him. "We're safe here. There is no one here to threaten us."

"What about these people? Who are they? Did you ask her?"

"Helen and Bob Darlon." I am relieved that he has come back to the present. "She said they were staying in a cabin not far from here. They left too late, the roads were iced and their car skidded and flipped over. They're just local people, I guess, who've run into bad luck."

"Swell, then they won't be a problem. As soon as the snow lets up we'll take him to a hospital. We'll move on then. We've been here too long already."

Helen shakily emerges from the bedroom. "He's going to die?"

she whispers to Gregory.

"I don't THINK his head injury is any more serious than a very bad concussion, But these are limited circumstances as you can see. So hard to tell with head injuries. There could be something I can't pick up from just a visual examination. But I think he will be all right. The best thing is just to keep him still until we can get him to a hospital."

She glances around again. "There is no way to a hospital?"

"No," Gregory says. "Not until the snow lets up."

"No way out?"

"I'm sorry," Gregory says. "There's no way out."

I try to smile at Helen. I know how she feels.

Stranded and trapped on an isolated mountaintop with her injured husband and strangers all around her. In this dreadful place she has joined us now- another caged animal.

Then the child sleepily climbs off the chair. "Daddy, come tuck me in. Read me a story."

"I'll look after your patient. I'll call you if he needs you." I set Gregory free to carry his child back to bed.

"Such a beautiful little girl," Helen says to me.

"She's just about perfect."

I let Helen sit on the chair. I perch on the fireplace hearth. Bob Darlon sleeps peacefully on the couch. The coal oil lamps burn steadily and the one near Helen gives her a soft radiance. I appreciate at this moment how much I have in common with this nice woman. I see her as a potential friend. I have not had a girlfriend in so very long.

"You're a nurse, I can tell," she says.

"I was until I got married."

"I know what you mean. When I married Bob I had every intention of sticking to my job but when my two boys came along, well, it was just too much to handle. How old is your little girl?"

"Barely three."

"And she's so precious. She looks just like your husband. And he is such a considerate father. Bob is good with our sons although he has such a demanding job. He's so ambitious and dedicated to his work. He hasn't much time to spend with them."

Reflexively we both study the injured man. To me he appears very much like Gregory was a few years ago. A young motivated man with all the promise of a good life before him. He has an intelligent face with sharp, strongly defined features.

In all probability he will recover from his injury and live happily for years with this congenial mother of his children.

I am not jealous of her. Indeed, I regard her as a fond reminder of how I once lived. She is like a photographic scene that triggers a beloved memory.

"What does your husband do?" I ask automatically.

"Bob is a private detective." She smiles proudly.

"A private detective?" I fear I am unable to keep the brittleness out of my voice.

Helen does not seem to notice,

"Yes, that's what we're doing up here. He's been trailing this one man for ages and the trail led up here to this ice box. We were supposed to go on vacation this month but then he gets a lead that the guy has been seen in this area."

"In this area?"

"Yes, so I just packed my bags and came along. Sometimes he stays gone for weeks at a time. So I said we'll just rent a cabin. You can look for this man during the day. We'll have evenings together. He wasn't too thrilled about the idea, but I talked him into it. I just wasn't going to give up another trip. We left the kids with my mother, of course."

"Of course." I am not visibly alarmed. I remain calm. Only all my blood is running up through my veins to my brain, causing my head to pound harder and harder as she talks on and on.

"Naturally," she adds, "I came along at my own expense, not his agency's. They don't even know I'm with Bob. You're up here on vacation too, I presume."

"On vacation."

"I figured as much."

"So this man your husband is after, who is he? What did he do?"

I ask as if the question did not really concern me.

Helen becomes even more gossipy. It is a relief to forget her own trouble by chatting about someone else's.

"Well, I don't know if you ever heard about it. It was on *The World News*. It happened almost two years ago in a small town. I think it was 76, or maybe late 1975? In Texas."

"In Texas?"

"In Texas there was a surgeon who had a patient who had an illegitimate baby, born previously. I'm not sure when, early 70s must have been, no, maybe it was 74? Whatever. Anyway, the mother of this child needed a simple appendectomy."

"An appendectomy?"

"Right. The surgeon's wife offered to keep the baby while the mother was in the hospital for the operation. And you won't believe this! While the woman was on the operating table, the surgeon murdered her!"

"Murdered her?"

"No one realized it until several hours after the woman died. No one had suspected that the surgeon was the child's real father. And later they found out the surgeon's wife couldn't have any babies of her own."

"No babies of her own."

I lean so close to the fire that the heat burns my skin. But it cannot warm me. I am too cold to ever be warm again.

"Did he really murder the woman on the operating table with so many others watching?" I ask as if I, too, love a good story,

In my mind I see a surgeon, masked, cutting, with just a flick of the eye to the nurse on the right and just a flick of the eye to the nurse on the left.

Then a hidden strategical slice.

"Isn't that amazing? He did it so skillfully that nobody knew what he was doing until later. After the woman died, a nurse realized what she had witnessed. They scheduled an autopsy. Before it was done, the surgeon and his wife had slipped away with the child."

"With the child."

"Ordinarily Bob's cases are so dull, you know the same old

thing over and over again, organized crime, dope peddlers, divorce, and the like. But this!"

I am not imagining it. Helen definitely speaks with admiration. Such a complicated crime of skill rouses in her a respect of sorts, secret sordid respect.

"The local police gave up tracking them a long time ago. But the dead woman's family hired Bob's agency to keep searching. Plus there is a reward."

"You- would you know this fugitive couple if you saw them?" I bite my lip.

I shouldn't have asked that. I am skating on thin ice,

But Helen merely frowns, seeking recollection. "I don't really remember. Bob has their photos, but, well, he's real real picky about my messing with his files, I learned years ago to leave his stuff alone, But I'm sure I would know them if I saw them. They must be evil looking people."

"Yes. Evil looking people." All this time I have been responding to her automatically, my mind has not been idle.

I know what must be done. I can see the sequence of events clearly.

I will go into the bedroom where Gregory sleeps with his child. Painfully, I will wake him. I will tell him. He will be stunned.

His patient is a predator. He is the prey.

I will see the same alarming desolation in his eyes that I have witnessed before.

I think back over all the time we have wasted running. Back over all the nights of fear. The nightmares. The days of doing without. Of hiding in small rat holes. The little disgusting jobs taken so we could eat. The single bedrooms with the child always between us at night.

The chill of slow self-destruction.

We are caught in the trap for infinity. The only moves allowed within its confines bring us closer to our demise.

What will be left of the man I loved and married if he kills again? Add more guilt to the burden he bears now and his very sanity will be in jeopardy. There will be no hope that we can ever go back to our past simple happiness.

I do not go into the bedroom. I do not tell him.

I have decided, I tell myself, to wait until dawn.

Gregory wakes up and comes back to the living room. "I didn't mean to go to sleep. I just fell asleep with the baby. Anna, you should have come and wakened me."

"He's been all right. He hasn't made a sound," I say.

"That's good," Gregory says to Helen. "You need to get some rest yourself."

"I should stay in here with Bob."

"There's no way to be comfortable in here." I say. "You need a good night's sleep. Your husband will need you when he wakes. Gregory and I will stay in here and watch him."

"Yes, I think it's best that I sleep in here just in case," says Gregory. "You can sleep with our little girl. You won't mind will you? There's only one bed."

"No of course not, but-"

"I'll make us a pallet on the floor."

I lead Helen to the bedroom. She is still protesting but only mildly. She is exhausted. As she sinks wearily on the bed, I vow to call her if there is any change. I envy her what little sleep she may snatch. I will have none.

I take the blankets to the living room.

"It feels so good to help somebody again. In a way it makes up for the past." Gregory sits cross-legged on the pallet.

I fix him a cup of coffee. I dissolve two Valium into the liquid before I hand him the cup. Valium is very effective on Gregory, making him sleep fast and deep. I am desperate for time alone to think what to do.

Half an hour later I ease into the bedroom. The child and Helen are asleep on the bed. The child is curled up against her. Helen holds this child tenderly in repose.

This child who is destroying so many lives.

Then I slip back into the living room. The coal oil lamp on the coffee table has burned out.

The other lamp and the smoldering fire give the scene an eerie glow.

I go to the window. The pane is still iced and cold to the touch. Now in total darkness I can no longer discern the white snow that pins us in this small cottage.

Gregory is breathing with a quiet rhythm, his relaxed face calling to mind the comfortable gentle life we once led.

I cannot let him kill again.

The sleeping detective appears less tranquil. He frowns slightly as if a sense of danger penetrates his subconscious. But he is defenseless, frozen in some enigmatic mental oblivion.

Gregory could not blame himself if his patient should have heart failure in his sleep. Unexpected death can come in a split second with a head injury.

I rifle through Gregory's medical case. As I prepare the lethal injection of digitalis, I think of Helen. She will not have to die if her husband does not wake up. His silence will save her life.

He stirs slightly as I give the injection.

He soon settles.

After, I lie down on the pallet beside Gregory and clasp his uncurled fingers tightly.

But I do not sleep.

I imagine that I can hear the snow falling. Each little crystal hits the roof with a little chime.

A hundred crystals drop each second as outside as it snows and snows and snows…

Ginger

By Deborah DR Kralich

Ginger Widdicombe took her name from her hair which was color of ginger spice. Her real name was Margaret Frances, but she was scarcely ever called that. Except by her mother, of course.

"Margaret Frances!"

"Yes, Mama?"

"Your father's home and supper's on the table."

"Yes, Mama."

"And I wish you'd learn to say something else besides 'yes, Mama'."

Ginger frowned. "All you do is gripe."

"Young lady, git in here right now before I kick you out of this house- lock, stock, and barrel. And go git Jerry."

Ginger's long legs stopped dangling from the porch. She debated on whether to bring them up onto the porch or let them slide down, taking the rest of her with them. She opted for the latter as it would take longer.

Inside the house her mother was alternately setting the table and taking up fried chicken. Her father was at the kitchen sink, washing his hands.

"I told you to go git Jerry."

"He'll come when he gets hungry enough."

"You're not going to let the boy go hungry just because you're too lazy to go and git him."

Jerry took this moment to slide through the door into the kitchen bringing dirt, grass, and dust with him. He immediately slipped and ended up sitting in the middle of the kitchen floor. Just as quickly he picked himself up and brushed off his pants, which made dust start flying around the room.

Ginger

Ginger coughed.

"Sorry, Gramma. Didn't mean to mess up your floor."

"That's all right. Ginger is goin' to help you clean it up and give you a bath."

"Like hell I am. You want him bathed, you bathe him."

"That's okay, Gramma. I don't need a bath. I'll just wash my hands real good."

"Don't tell me you don't need a bath. You're as filthy as a pig."

"Aw, Gramma!"

"To the bathroom, march!"

Above Jerry's screams and his grandma's griping, Ginger and her father ate wordlessly.

Ginger bore an amazing resemblance to her father. Charlie Martin was a tall slim man possessing the same ginger spice hair and keen piercing blue eyes.

Ginger's keen piercing blue eyes were her only feature that gave a clue to her real age. Ginger viewed life as a merry-go-round and without make-up, which she never wore, she could easily pass for 16.

She was 27.

"What are we goin' to do with you, Ginger?"

"I don't know, Daddy." What an odd time to remember that he had given her that nickname.

"Then you're gonna have to get you a husband, girl."

"And almost thirty year old divorcee with a six year old brat in a small town. What kind of husband could I catch?"

"Go to Dallas."

"Done caught one husband there. Don't want no more like him, thank you."

"Well, San Antonio, then."

"I've been to San Antonio. It's all old. It is decaying. Ain't nothing there for young people."

"First you're old. Now you're young. You don't know what you are. Besides, what's here for young people? Houston's alive and modern. Go there. You can't find nothing wrong with it."

"I'd have to take Jerry."

"Yeah, you'd have to take Jerry. You might as well face it, girl, you've got a son. You're responsible for him. Lots of other women have children and it don't ruin their lives. Even if they do have to raise them alone. They look on them as a blessing, something to live for."

Ginger suppressed a wild urge to laugh.

Then before she could reply, in came the object of their conversation, spanking clean from head to toe, with noticeable red ears. Grandma was right behind him.

"Grampa, she practically drowned me."

"Don't bother your grandpa. Sit down, shut up, and eat your supper."

"He wasn't bothering me, Ruthie."

"I can't shut up and eat my supper too, Gramma. I have to open my mouth to eat."

At this outrageous insolence, his grandma reached and slapped him so hard that he lost his balance and nearly fell out of his chair.

"You didn't have to do that, Ruthie." Charlie's voice never went beyond its normal tone. And he never pressed an issue twice with his wife. Therefore, she largely ignored him.

"Ginger, git over there and clean up the mess he made."

"Daddy was talking to you, Mama."

"I heard him and you heard me. Now git to work."

Ginger stood up so quickly her chair fell over. "Dammit, I didn't make that mess. Jerry did. Make him clean it up."

"I just gave him a bath. Now you– "

"It's okay, Gramma, I'll clean it up." Whereupon his grandma gave him the same treatment as before, only on the other cheek. Jerry wanted to cry but he knew better. Grandma didn't allow it.

"I didn't make any mess. I'm not cleaning any up."

Charlie picked up Jerry and quietly slipped outside. They sat on the porch, Ginger's refuge, and Jerry cried quietly on his grandpa's shoulders.

Inside Ruthie's shouting grew louder. "You're lazy and no good for nothing. We're supporting you and the kid and you won't even take care of him. He sees more of me than of you. You're gone all night and you sleep all day. When you're not sleeping, you're on the phone or you're sitting on the back porch playing with caterpillars and cockroaches."

Ginger flew out the door. Finding the porch occupied, she proceeded to the backwoods that ran in a stretch of 2 miles, part of which landed at the foot of the hill on which the house was built. Picking her way through it carefully she soon found the climbable comfortable tree that she had discovered when she was 10. Nobody knew about this tree, not even her father. She only went there in panic or desperation to reduce the risk of it being found. It was her private place to think and be alone.

She did not want to think right now. She couldn't help it. She tried not to think of her ex-husband but his face kept popping up in all the leaves and on all the branches. There was even a huge image of him on the tree trunk. And when she tried to block them out by closing her eyes, she could see him perfectly down to the smallest detail. His light brown hair, his big blue mischievous eyes, his deep tan, his beautiful smile– getting wider, laughing.

Laughing at her? No, he never seemed to be. But of course she knew now he had been. Laughing when he proposed. Laughing because he knew she loved him so much. Laughing because she was a small country girl who had never been outside of Texas. Because she was bewildered by Dallas and dazzled by Six Flags. That was where he proposed. On the merry-go-round, on the white horse with pink and purple saddle. He would love her forever and ever and they would spend their life laughing at the world. They eloped (she remembered that he laughed at the wedding too) and they went to Malibu.

For two glorious years they lived in a romantic paradise there. He never worked but she was too happy to wonder where the money came from. Then some friends of theirs had a baby and he wanted one, too. Ginger had been wary of the idea. She really did not like kids. He alternately pleaded and threatened.

At first it was 'darling think our own flesh and blood'.

The idea of a son enchanted him. But he soon phased out the pleading and they argued frequently.

Because she was afraid to lose him she finally let him have his way.

His enrapture with Jerry lasted exactly one month. The first time Jerry threw up all over him, he threw the child on the bed and never touched him again.

Soon he began to go out 'with the boys'. If he would come home and all he would be drunk. Then he would sleep all day, and if the baby cried, he went into a mad rage that sometimes lasted for weeks.

But he was still the same in bed. When they left the baby with other people it was almost as if the child had never been born. So she was shocked when he came home one night with a petite blonde hippie and presented her with divorce papers. If she signed, he would give them plane fare back to Dallas. If not, he would just walk away and leave them there without a dime.

She knew she had no choice but she told him to leave and come back in the morning. She cried all night long, along with the baby.

When he came back, she signed and he gave her the money. She hitchhiked from Dallas to her parents' home knowing that back in Malibu his laughter was getting louder with every mile.

So here she was five years later sitting in a tree still moping about it. The absurdity of the situation dawned on her and she smiled. Promptly the multi-pictures of her ex-husband disappeared and the tree became a tree again.

Ginger sighed. It was getting very dark. She looked at the tree. Definitely a tree, no pictures anywhere. Time to go home. She walked down slowly, reluctantly.

Snakes were nondiscriminating and Ginger was not wearing tennis shoes. She tripped once and grabbed a tree for support she was completely startled when the tree grabbed hold of her. She looked up seeing rather long black hair and an enchantingly cute smile.

"Hello." The stranger in the woods could not seem to think of anything else to say.

Ginger frowned. "You're not local," she said accusingly.

"No. I'm from Houston. My name is Jerry Price."

"Jerry? I've got a son named Jerry."

"You've got a son?" There was a cute smile again. "That doesn't seem reasonable."

"I'm 27," Ginger said indignantly.

"Oh. You and your husband live around here?"

"I'm divorced." Ginger started walking again.

"Well, what's your name?" He was right beside her.

"Ginger Mm- Widdicombe."

"Where do you live, Ginger? I may call you Ginger, I presume."

"Oh sure. See the house up there? I live there with my parents and Jerry. What are you doing in the East Texas woods?"

"I'm a photographer. I'm up here practicing my trade."

She noted the camera. "You make much money doing that?"

"I make a living. And I enjoy it."

They were almost at her home. "You like to come in?"

"If I'm not imposing."

"Oh, no."

She started up the steps ahead of him.

"Stop," he said. "Turn around."

She did so involuntarily and he photographed her. On the porch of the old frame house in shorts and without makeup. For the longest time she stood there debating whether to laugh at him or belt him one. Then he smiled again and she knew she was not going to do either.

"Margaret Frances!"

"Someone calling you?"

"Oh, come on." She called inside, "Mama, we've got company. This is Jerry Price, a photographer from Houston."

Ruthie Martin eyed him suspiciously. "Another Jerry, huh? You sure are good at bringing them home." Then to Price, "you're too late for supper but there's some cold chicken in the icebox."

"I hadn't planned-"

"And you're welcome to stay the night."

Jerry Price stayed the night, the next night, and the next week. He decided, he said, to make a photographic study of a country family. He paid Charlie Martin $15 a day and helped him with the yard work. He took pictures at random and soon they grew used to the clicking. Most of the time his camera focused on Ginger. Her childlike personality enchanted him and he was determined to capture it on film.

As time went on, Ginger became more and more annoyed. She told herself the cause of her discontent was the constant surveillance and clicking she was subjected to. However, the real reason was that while Price was taking hundreds of pictures of her, he was ignoring her in every other way. He made no advances, passionate or otherwise, and when he was not photographing, he was not around.

Ginger soon decided to hell with it all and told Price to get lost in no uncertain terms.

He reacted the usual way. He smiled and took a picture. Then he smiled some more.

Ginger was enraged. She picked up a rock and threw it at him. He ducked and took another picture. Ginger then tried unceremoniously to punch him in the mouth. She missed and landed in a brush pile. And he took another picture.

He reached to help her out. She grabbed him by the wrist and pulled him in the brush pile, camera and all. He sat there stunned for a moment. Then he started laughing and she began to laugh, too. He was equally stunned when she suddenly stopped laughing and flew to the house.

In the brush pile Ginger had suddenly stopped laughing because she had suddenly stopped loving her ex-husband and started loving Jerry Price. It was a new situation and ever since her marriage, Ginger was extremely wary of new situations. Especially ones which involved falling in love with big brown eyes and cute smiles.

Later Ginger would wonder what Jerry Price thought that day. If he read her feelings, he gave no sign. Indeed, he was more elusive than ever. Yet he prolonged his stay for another week and shadowed Ginger constantly. Conversation among them was almost nonexistent. Only in the backwoods did he open up to her. He would walk beside her, his camera strapped over his shoulder, their hands rarely touching. She soon learned to walk beside him in silence.

Occasionally they would leave the worn trail and climb various hills or trees. She would sit in his arms or he would lounge on the ground. She would put his head on her lap and run her finger through his hair.

When he did talk, he talked of photography, his plans to go to Northern Ireland to photograph the war. The subject did not particularly please Ginger for it reminded her that eventually he would leave and so far he showed no desire to take her with him.

They first made love in the woods. In contrast to his solitary cautious ways he made love brutally savagely thrusting himself upon her. often leaving her bruised and exhausted. She gave in to him eagerly though and always initiated their intercourse. She loved him more now than she had ever loved her husband. She began to wonder if she had ever really cared for her husband. When she thought of Jerry's father, he seemed far away, as much in the past as her first grade teacher. The real world with all its problems, promises and people became superficial while the superficial world in the woods became real.

When he took her out socially, which was rarely, he was an entirely different person. He became once more the charming charismatic young man who first greeted her in the woods. She began to believe he was two different men. An impetuous loner and a gregarious charmer. He could be one or the other or both.

Despite the uncertainty of the affair, Ginger was oddly content. Only the nagging fear that he would leave irritated her but she resolutely shoved that thought out of her mind and soon it dared not enter. Her parents became plastic fixtures in her world and her son's existence in the mind of his mother, precarious to begin with, vanished entirely from her surrealistic environment.

Contrary to what Ginger expected, Jerry Price got along famously with her mother and her son. After Price had been with them a week or so Ruthie Martin even begin to drop subtle hints that he would be most welcome as a son-in-law. Young Jerry, exposed to a young male adult for the first time in his life, began to hero worship Price to the point of imitating him in every possible way. Only Charlie Martin had reservations about this young demagogue.

"What does he do for a living," Charlie would often ask

Ginger.

"He shoots pictures, Daddy," she would patiently reply.

"But child that's not work."

"Yes, it is Daddy. It's a respectable profession."

"Who pays him? Where does he get the money he's paying me for board?"

"He got it from his last assignment. Photographers get paid a lot all at one."

"So do bank robbers."

Ginger realized that neither of her parents had the faintest idea there was a sexual relationship between her and Price. They both took great pains to hide that aspect. Ginger also realize she could get pregnant. However it was sometime before she found courage to suggest he use a condom. He laughed.

"Don't you see I can't use nothing?" she said heatedly. "Mama would find out."

"Don't worry sweetie. I had a vasectomy."

"Of what?"

"The operation to make me sterile."

"Oh, yeah, I knew they had such things but I didn't know the name for them. You don't want kids?"

He shook his head.

"I never could see much sense in having kids."

"Really! I can't either!" Ginger was pleased that he shared her views.

"Why did you have Jerry then?"

She told him everything.

"That's a terrible thing to do to a woman." He looked angry.

"I loved him." Ginger shrugged. "I love you now."

He looked at her for a long moment.

"Do you?"

"Why Jerry, you should know."

"Yeah but you never said so right out."

"Well I do."

"Ginger, we had an interesting relationship these past few months but I never dreamed you took it seriously." He looked slightly alarmed.

Ginger felt like she had been slapped hard.

"I slept with you," she said, making an effort to control impending tears.

"Yeah but-" He left the sentence hanging.

"But what?" She got up off the ground. "What have you been doing with me? Playing games? You think I'm a toy?"

"Now, don't get upset."

"You men, you're all bastards. It's all been for those damn pictures hasn't it? Hasn't it?"

He rose and patted her head sympathetically.

"You asked for it. You practically threw yourself at me every time." He sounded defensive.

Ginger reeled. She knew he was not lying. She could not bring herself to call him a liar.

He took a deep breath. "I'm a photographer and a professional. I'm on assignment now to photograph country people and country living. I found the perfect subject. A beautiful young naïve country girl who had been exposed to but left perfectly untouched by the outside world. Even giving birth to a son didn't move her to change her ways."

"I'm not a country girl. I'm nothing like any of them," Ginger protested.

"Oh but you are!" He looked almost inspired. "There has always been low morality in the country for divorced women. But I bet you were a virginal bride."

She glared in confused anger. "You son of a bitch!"

"You want nothing more than to be married. And you want children. Oh yes you do! The only reason you have rejected little Jerry is because your husband rejected him. Little Jerry did not please your husband. Your husband was the one person who mattered, so there must be something wrong with little Jerry."

Ginger shook her head dazedly. Tears began to stream down her face.

Jerry Price grabbed her by the shoulders.

"Don't you see why I did it?" His eyes glistened. "You're

perfect. You'll never change. You're the prototype of a country girl wronged. You're untouchable!

Ginger raised her head up with dignity.

"You touched me."

Price began to walk in a small circle.

"I guess I better go on and leave now before this gets any more out of hand."

"That's why you were always so silent when we were alone. Because you had nothing to say. You were just pretending."

"I would not have made love to you if you hadn't thrown yourself at me. But it added something. Ginger, I could write a book about you. You fascinate me."

"As a subject."

"Yes."

"You are right. You had better leave now."

Ginger almost cried with relief when they returned to the house and found it empty. She sat on the back porch while Price gathered his few things. He did not bother to come out and say goodbye. She knew when he left only because she heard the front door slam.

Some hours later Ginger was still sitting on the porch when her mother and Jerry came home.

"Margaret, where are you at?" Ruthie called.

"I'm on the porch, Mama."

"Where's your young man?"

"He's gone."

"What?"

"He's gone," she shouted.

Ruthie walked outside. Her daughter was sprawled on the porch, feet dangling off. Ruthie opened her mouth then closed it. Something about the expression in Ginger's dry blue eyes made her skip a lecture on laziness that she often delivered at such times.

"Why did he leave?"

Ginger sat up. She felt no explanation was owed, especially to her mother.

"It was just time for him to go."

For the second time Ruthie bit back a lecture. She had a sudden strong desire that Ginger confide in her so she could hold and comfort her. Ginger said nothing. Ruthie went back into the house.

In a minute though Jerry walked out on the porch and sat down beside his mother. Ginger ignored him. He sat there a while fiddling with a wooden whistle Charlie had made him.

"Ginger," he said finally.

She looked at him blandly.

"Why did Jerry Price leave?"

"He had other places to go."

"Where?"

"Paris, I think." Ginger sniffed. "Or Ireland."

"Gee, I wish he would have taken us with him."

Ginger started to cry but the little boy seemed not to notice.

"I'm sure going to miss him."

Ginger jumped off the porch. She ran towards the woods, tears streaming down her cheeks.

For a moment the boy sat there fiddling with the whistle. Then in a gesture of anger and frustration he hurled the toy as far as his small arm could throw it towards the woods.

Ginger got halfway to her tree when she stopped short. Inexplicably she did not want to go there. She turned in confusion. Then with a sickening feeling she remembered her son's wide-eyed face as he asked why his friend was gone. She felt, for the first time, empathy for her son. And she felt lonely.

Charlie Martin arrived home from work that evening an hour late. His wife greeted him with the news that Jerry Price was gone.

"Good," he commented gruffly.

"We needed that money." Ruthie sounded exasperated. "Ginger should've kept him here."

"Anyway she could?"

Their eyes met in confrontation. For the first time in many years Ruthie's dropped to the floor first. Charlie let opportunity slide.

"Where is she?"

"On the porch. In the woods. I don't know." Ruthie slammed the cabinet door in frustration.

Charlie went outside and with difficulty sat down on the porch steps beside his daughter.

"So he's gone."

"Yup, he's gone."

Charlie put his arms around Ginger. She leaned gratefully on his shoulder.

"Were you in love with him?"

"I think. Yes, I was."

Charlie's sigh was a combination of sympathy and frustration.

"Child, you don't even know who he really was."

Ginger was amazed at her father's astuteness. She could not reply.

"What now, child?"

She looked up quickly. "I've been thinking."

"Yes?"

She looked up quickly.

"About what you said. About Houston. But- " She lowered her eyes again.

"But Jerry?"

"Yes Jerry," she agreed in a small voice.

"You have to take him, girl. That's all there is to it. He is yours."

"But does he know that? Does he understand I'm his mother? Does he know what that means? Would he go with me?" She halfway hoped for a negative reply.

"He comprehends a lot more than you think. Talk to him."

"You talk to him, Daddy," she pleaded.

"You have to face him sooner or later."

"I can't," she said desperately.

"You must," he replied simply.

Charlie left his daughter alone once more. He felt with a father's unique feeling of helplessness that he had done all he could do for Ginger. The rest was up to her. She would have to take her own steps in life if she were ever to have one of her own. The idea fluttered across his mind that if Ruthie was a different type person, Ginger might have worked things out long ago. He dismissed the notion at once. Ruthie had been a good wife to him in some pretty hard times. She deserved his loyalty now that she was old.

It was dark outside by now. Ginger was watching the stars. Her head swam when she tried to picture what had happened in the last two months. She had the vague feeling of being wronged but somehow she did not blame Jerry Price as she had blamed her husband years ago.

She had a premonition that the hurt of losing Jerry Price was as surrealistic as their affair had been and would not last long in her mind. Her son weighed heavily on her mind for the first time since she had returned to the country. She was literally terrified of the idea of asking him if he would like to go with her the same way he had wanted to go with Price. Yet she knew it was ridiculous that a grown woman was afraid of a seven year old boy.

At least he wanted to go somewhere. They had that in common.

It struck her that that was the second time she had found something in common with her son in a few hours after six years of unfamiliarity.

She walked slowly in the house. It was 8 PM and her parents and Jerry were in bed. She eased into Jerry's room and closed the door.

"Gramma?"

"No, it's me."

"Oh, Ginger, it's you."

"Yeah. Hey, can I turn on the light?"

"Sure."

Ginger flipped on a lamp and sat down on the bed. Jerry propped himself up with a pillow. He was waiting expectantly.

"Uh," said Ginger.

"Huh?"

"Jerry, can we sorta have a man to man talk?" She smiled nervously.

"Sure."

Ginger gulped. *Here goes*, she thought.

"You know I'm your mama? I'm the person responsible for you. Not Gramma or Grampa."

There was a long silence. The boy looked serious but the question did nothing to upset him.

Ginger was relieved. She had expected a scene, or at least tears.

"Yes'm."

"Um- I- uh, figure I'll be goin' to Houston tomorrow or maybe the day after. You want to go?"

"You mean for a visit? A trip?" The boy was wide eyed.

"Well, no. We'd live there."

"With who?" He looked confused.

"With no one. I'd get a job. We could live in an apartment. Your granddad would give us a little money to live on till I found something." Ginger was trying to explain.

"Oh, well, I don't know." He spoke hesitantly, then a little hopefully. "We'd live together?"

Ginger smiled. "Of course. Just us- Ginger and Jerry Widdicombe."

Jerry sniffed hard. "Well, in that case, I guess I'll go."

Suddenly he jumped and put his arms around her neck.

"Good," she replied, gently pulling them off. "We'll talk more about it in the morning." Ginger turned out the light. She felt better.

"Good night. Mama." He smiled hesitantly.

"Good night, Jerry."

Ginger slipped out onto the porch again. She was not sure how she felt about her son yet. She seriously doubted they would ever have a typical mother-son relationship but she was pretty sure things would work out in Houston. She wondered if any of her high school secretarial skills were still with her, resting dormant. She remembered Price had said he was from Houston. It would be funny if they met in his city. But she thought wryly, he probably been lying about that, too.

Ginger felt emotionally exhausted and it was getting chilly. The bright stars were yielding to clouds. Ginger was tired. She walked sleepily in the house and went to bed.

The Wounded Man

By Deborah DR Kralich

The vinyl seat was cold and it groaned as she slid her naked legs under the wheel.

The car would not start. Her bare foot pumped the gas. The motor slovenly whirred at the flick of the key.

At last it turned over and she raced the engine. She coughed as the exhaust fumes rose up against her. She looked at the kitchen door, expecting it to burst open any minute. It remained closed. She jerked the gearshift into reverse and shot backwards out of the garage.

It was the dead of night. As she turned out of the driveway, a few neon rays fell on her freckled arms which jutted from her body and braced against the steering wheel. She glanced down at her breasts barely covered by the nearly sleeveless top and her legs shielded only by straying strings from her cotton cutoff jeans.

She was cold.

She switched a knob to red but the car was not yet warm and the heater threw cold air at her.

She turned it back off.

Suddenly she was trying to get on the freeway. The freeway was over 3 miles from her home. Her skin was iced. She put the heater on. Warmth flowed into the car. Where had her mind vanished to? It had died. A corner of her mouth turned up as she mentally wrote the obituary notice for the newspaper:

PATTERSON, Mrs. June (mind)
The mind of Mrs. June Patterson, 28, of 1151 Oakdale

The Wounded Man

entered into rest around 11 PM on October 10, 1978.
Survived by one body- a Mrs. June Patterson, 28,
1151 Oakdale, services will be held-

Her thoughts sank in the drenching sound of a horn coming from behind. The bright lights of a truck beamed into her rearview mirror.

She twisted her neck and peered over her left shoulder.

That crazy truck driver. Couldn't he see all those cars coming? Her little Impala would be smashed to bits if she pulled out in front of them.

She lifted her foot from the brake and let the car roll off the entrance ramp onto the shoulder of the freeway.

The truck jumped angrily around her.

He could take such careless chances, with a safe secure seat in a big cab and Lord knows how many feet loaded behind him.

She watered the windshield and turned on the wiper to clean it. At last there were no oncoming headlights. She was able to pull on to the expressway.

She relaxed as she drove firmly along the straight highway.

She liked driving best when she was the only traveler on the road. But when she looked in the mirror she saw a wolf pack approaching rapidly. On Highway 59 cars traveled in wolf packs. A few minority cars, driving the speed limit or less, drew like honey draws flies, race drivers that hounded their tails and wavered and weaved their way through the pack, breaking out in front, finally racing 90 miles an hour the short distance to the next bottleneck. The safest way to drive was to try to stay in the free space between the packs.

This wolf pack was coming fast. She slowed to 35 and forced her eyes straight ahead until they flew around her.

She sped up again as their red tail lights disappeared.

She was passing the city. The drab dull daytime city was so beautiful at night. It was lit up like a giant old-fashioned county fair. How nice not having to worry about getting to the opposite side of the freeway and exiting to town.

She had the freedom of sailing straight down, down, flat, flat on the ground. The tires humming as they swallowed up the dim gray cement.

From overhead a thousand shadows cast a continuous flicker over her skin. The network of overpasses was like ribbons about to float away into the sky.

Passing underneath, she made the car go faster. The automobile shot over the pavement like a speedboat over smooth lake water.

She turned on the radio, punching the buttons to find a hard rock station. No country and western tonight. The volume rose. Ear splitting, mind grinding, brain jolting music.

Music that could cause sexual ecstasy.

She broke out in a sweat.

Then her mind broke free and she rode on the vibration.

Her body still drove the car but her mind floated on the crashing music. It drifted past the populated north side of Houston, out further and further.

The bright lights of the city were gone and vacant lands and woods stretched all around her like a great big menacing bear.

She was lost.

She was frightened.

She had been abandoned.

How long had she been away from home?

No, she did not want to think of home.

Forget home.

Forget home exists.

Ah, there was a saving sight. Police lights flashed just a few feet down the road. She speeded up to get to them.

The policeman was parked on the side of the road alone with his light spinning around and around.

She pulled her car in behind his and got out.

The fall night was clear and cool. Gravel rolled under her bare feet causing them to sting.

As she approached the police car she was conscious of silence.

The motor was eerily dead.

The policeman appeared to be asleep, his head resting against the window.

How stupid of him, she thought, to go to sleep with his light still flashing.

She knocked on the window as she peered inside.

The policeman did not respond...

She could not hardly see inside the car in the darkness. The blue, white, and red circling about her made her eyes hurt.

She rapped harder. Suddenly a blue beam fell down on the policeman's hand, clinched against his stomach, the fingers streaked with blood. His hand was white contrasted to his dark uniform. Then the hand became bluish, then reddish, then white again... fleshy, striped white...

She jerked at the handle.

The door opened and she jumped back as the man began to slide out. She knew she could just not stand there idly as he fell. He would be hurt further, his head would hit the concrete. She ran two steps to him, squatted and caught him in her arms before he hit the pavement.

She was aware that in her arms was a quivering living human being. A nice looking young man, limp like the blades of grass growing along the highway. He moaned.

As she struggled to get him back into the car and on the seat, his eyes flew open in terror. He stared at her weakly in fear and pain, then his lips moved.

She did not understand him.

"It's all right," she said, caressing his damp forehead. "I'm a friend. It's all right. I won't hurt you"

She was sure he relaxed a little. She was almost on top of him in the front seat of the patrol car.

"Call for help," he said, with difficultly. "Please."

"How?" She knelt in the small floorboard space on the passenger side. "Tell me how!"

He made a strong effort to regain full consciousness. He was able to instruct her on how to use his radio.

"Hello! Hello!" She shouted into it. "Is anyone there? Is

anyone there? Please, there's this policeman who has been wounded. Please, we need an ambulance now! We need it now!"

"Where are you? Where are you?" A crackling computer-like reply demanded their location.

"Oh, I don't know. Way outside of Houston, 59 North. I don't know. The lights are flashing. Two cars parked and the lights are flashing."

She dropped the radio and began to cry. The young policeman raised his hand to calm her. She saw tranquility in his eyes.

"Okay," he whispered. "Good."

He was in pain and it was getting worse for him. She grasped his shoulders and he shivered, clutching her arms. He strove to keep quiet and still.

He bit his lip and tried to smile at her.

"Scream," she told him. "Scream and kick if it hurts. Maybe it won't hurt so badly if you scream."

"What's your name?" He struggled to talk.

"June."

"Dav- David."

"Married? June?"

"Yes."

She thought he was probably trying to switch his mind away from the pain. He pulled her close to him.

"Husband with you- June?"

"No. Don't talk about that. I mean don't try so hard to talk."

"Me, too. I just got married, just last week."

"Oh," she said, beginning to cry again. "Oh, David."

His name came out of her mouth as easily as her own.

"June. Talk to me, June. Please. "

"I'm 28," she said idiotically.

He was going to speak but instead he grabbed his stomach and screamed. She bent and pressed her cheek to his, holding him to her tightly, shamelessly, for they were the only two people in the world under that deadly carousel of lights.

"David. David, don't die. Hang on David. They'll be here soon. Look David. See how I'm breathing, breathe like me. Deep, in and out. In, out. In. Out. Hold my hand tighter. Hang on David hang on."

"June," he gasped. "June, June, June, June June!"

"Yes dear. I'm here. I'm June."

"Oh. Oh, June."

"David, David. Pray to God. Let's pray to God to save your life."

"Dear God, please please! I don't want-I don't want to die. Dear-God..."

"God, she said. "Please don't let David die. God, please don't let this person die."

"June, oh June!"

"They'll be here in a minute. In just a minute."

"Who?" The pain subsided for a second and David managed a small grin. "The cops, or God, or the devil?"

"The ambulance, it will get here soon."

He doubled up again. "Oh, oh, oh, God, please, please."

She pressed her whole body against him as well as she could in the car.

"I'm cold," he said. "I'm cold."

His hand flattened stiffly against the car seat. She pried it loose and grasped it. She felt something hard and cold and flat among his fingers. She visualized steel.

Then it came to her not steel, but gold.

"What's your wife's name? David?"

"What? Huh? June?"

"I'm here. I'm June."

"Oh, it's, uh, Nannette. Oh, dear God. June."

His arm clutched her breast. She put her head back down against him.

David and Nannette. She silently coupled the names, all the while staring at the black floorboard. David and Nannette.

Suddenly there was someone lunging into the car.

A strong man restrained her as other men picked up David and carried him away.

"Don't hurt him again," she said. "Not again. Don't hurt him again."

"Relax, lady. We're taking him to a hospital. Did you see what happened? Did you see anything?"

She was dragged out of the car and the cool night air hit her again. There seem to be a million red, white, and blue flashing lights filling all of the space around and above her with sparkling multicolor fire.

"I have to go to the hospital with David. I have to. I have to."

One policeman looked at his partner.

"She's in shock," said one.

"Let's take her in our car," said the other.

The policemen talked calmly to her all the way to the medical center. They thought at first she could not remember but she remembered everything. Only what could she tell them? She had just found him.

At the hospital she waited with the policeman in a little room just in view of the hallway where David occupied a gurney. She glimpsed him, prone, motionless, inert, covered with a white sheet.

Medical personnel fluttered around him, then took him away.

The policemen beside her told her that they were David's friends. They had known David a long time.

They took down her name, address, and phone number.

How long had she known David?

"Never before. I did not know him," she said. "Not before."

She felt warm and safe with the policemen. The little room was like a cozy haven. She remembered feeling that way before, although it seemed so long ago...

Where was she when she had felt so warm before? She buried her head in her hands as she tried to recall. At work? No. At home? No it could not have been at home. She must not think about home.

The policeman suddenly all left.

She was alone again.

She was more alone than before she began her late-night ride.

She walked to the narrow doorway...

The policemen stood in the hall with more policemen forming a protective ring around a thin young woman. All their attention focused.

Did they not know that someone else cried for David as well?

She had no handsome men in blue to comfort her.

She felt lost and abandoned again. She belonged nowhere. Not with these people who waited for David nor at home.

No, she would not think of home. Not home.

Only victims lived at her home.

A wounded woman and a wounded man.

She went into the hall. They were talking quietly.

Then the girl saw her. "Oh, thank you." She broke away from the group. "Thank you for finding David. And for helping him. The doctor says you found him in time. What were you doing so far out, so late at night in the middle of nowhere?"

No answer came. She froze.

The young woman stepped back guiltily as if she were afraid she had said the wrong thing to someone she owed so much.

"I had a fight with my husband..."

"We don't need you anymore," said a policeman. "Your husband has been called and he is coming to get you. You can go on home with him when he gets here."

"Go home and make up with him," said the young frightened bride. "Go and tell him that fight saved my husband's life."

"I will, Nannette. I will." She took the younger girl's hand.

"You know my name? He called my name?" Her voice held the excited insecurity of a newlywed. "He called for me? He called my name?"

"Oh yes," said June, her voice rising with certainty. "He called it over and over and over again."

Ghost Stories

By Deborah DR Kralich

Adrienne grasped a tree for support as she fought her way over the brush covered trail.

"Charles' first wife haunts these very woods."

"Ghost stories." There was scorn in Candy's light voice.

She negotiated the same dense forest with effortless dexterity.

"I've heard it from more than one person," insisted Adrienne, resting against the antique four trunk oak, which stood in a ringed clearing as if no other growth dared approach. The unique landmark signaled the end of the man-made trail. Beyond was an almost impassable mass of solid greenery.

"Ghost stories." Candy, remaining amidst the thick bushes, shook her head in disgust.

"Patricia walks these woods at night and weeps for Charles. Her golden curls glisten in the moonlight as she floats above the trees." Adrienne was trying to convey horror to break the teen's composure.

She failed.

"Floats above the trees? Ridiculous," said Candy, a box of chocolates materializing in her hand. "Those who are telling those stories just want to drive you away from the ranch."

Adrienne had encountered her new friend a week ago. Informed that she had strayed onto the private property of the Double C Ranch, Candy had expressed exaggerated dismay. She offered an insincere humorous apology, disdaining a 'Trespassers Will Be Shot' billboard.

Adrienne liked Candy at once, giving assurances as the ranch's future mistress that she would make sure Candy could hike all she wanted.

Adrienne had better not pull her weight until officially titled such, Candy had replied. Adrienne had laughed, but prudently agreed. Her fiancé, Charles Welder, and his sister, Crisha, long the dominant forces at the Double C, habitually monopolized everyone and everything crossing into the ranch's boundaries.

Adrienne and Candy began meeting for daily forays. Adrienne needed the workouts physically and mentally. Candy seemed to be just having fun.

"I shall be so glad when I master the art of traipsing through dense forest and never mussing a hair." Adrienne dug her fingers into her auburn hair, now a tangled mess after catching on several low hanging limbs.

"Practice," said Candy, her blond coiffure picture-perfect. "Remember I've been used to Texas terrain all my life. 18 years."

"I know we have not mentioned our personal lives since we became hiking buddies, but I just need someone to talk to about all this. And if you came to the house- "

"I've no desire to visit you at the ranch house. I've been there. Not impressed."

"Do you know Charles then?"

Candy popped a chocolate covered cherry in her mouth, then offered the small box of confections to Adrienne, who declined impatiently.

"I am going to be as thin as possible on my wedding day."

"I knew Charles Welder. Rich boy of the county. My sisters were entranced, but too young for him," said Candy, with hesitation. "Many don't remember all us Snell girls. Seven of us. All blond, born stairstep in the sixties. Each looking like the other. We confuse people."

"I was born in 1958."

"So you are 25."

"Eight years younger than Charles, I'm his equal in maturity, I assure you. Along with the beginning of my wedded life shortly, this momentous year of 1983 heralds the end days of my first quarter century." Adrienne stretched, feeling triumphant for a moment.

"It will be dark soon." Candy pocketed the chocolates.

"Just a minute more rest."

Adrienne wanted to keep Candy on the subject of Charles Welder before interest waned in what the teen probably considered the ancient past.

"So back then, in the 1970s, about Charles? Did you tag along when your older sisters hung around with him?"

"Charles- hmm- up above it all, you know? When he was growing up here his folks didn't want him associating too much with the peasants."

"Know anything about Patricia? The mystery woman no one will talk to me about. Except to say her ghost is preparing to waylay me some dark and dreary night." Adrienne impatiently snapped a branch. "I don't know what to make of it all."

"Yes. I recall Patricia." Candy's tone was compassionate, a little pity for one who does not know all the facts.

Adrienne's voice became rushed, desolate. "I know you were just a kid but did you ever meet her? Who was she? Why is her name anathema to Charles? Why is her picture never seen? Why has she such a hold over this town and this ranch?"

"I remember. He met her at the county fair." Candy smiled nostalgically and nibbled on another dark rich chocolate. Her voice halted, frustrating Adrienne unbearably.

"Tell me about her, please. No one will say how she died. Her name is not spoken. There isn't a picture of her in the house. Not even a wedding picture. The first day I arrived I saw an empty frame on Charles' bureau in his bedroom. I want to look for the missing photo but I'm relegated to a guest room until after the wedding. Crisha watches us like a hawk. If one of us goes near the other's bedroom she's right there between us no matter what time of day or night." Adrienne sighed.

"Old morality dies hard here." Candy chuckled. "Charles' first wife is no longer important. You are important now. You have so much power in your hands."

"No, I'm helpless. Helpless." Adrienne crumpled against the massive four trucked oak in despair.

"Listen, Adrienne." Candy squatted down beside her. "You have the power to help Charles. He's suffered. Everyone around here knows how much. The Bible says we suffer. Yet not always. Suffering should end sometime."

"A-dren? A-dren de-ar? Where are you? Suppertime!"

"Oh, no," said Adrienne. "Crisha's calling."

"I am familiar with her all right. My name is anathema to her. She's the real reason I'd just as soon avoid social interaction with your set. Just ignore her for a second, and listen to me." Candy gazed directly at Adrienne. A strong persuasive force emanated from Candy's emerald green eyes. "Ignore these ghost stories. Concentrate on your future with Charles. Don't let the past ruin you. Don't believe ghost stories."

"Candy- " Adrienne stopped short of telling Candy the truth.

Adrienne had to believe the ghost stories.

Adrienne had seen the ghost herself.

"Got to go."

Candy went the opposite direction, plunging into the greenery.

Behind Adrienne came a crashing lumbering sound. The brush gave way, cracking and groaning, as Crisha clomped into view.

"You should not be alone in these woods."

Crisha panted as she came upon Adrienne.

"I was with a friend," said Adrienne, wondering why those words sounded defiant.

Candy, some distance away now, glanced back and waved.

Crisha peered.

"Who's she?" Carrying her bulk through the forest rendered Crisha barely able to speak.

"One of the Snell girls." Annoyed at being fetched by Crisha, Adrienne swiftly made her way back towards the clearing, without regard for the larger woman's fatigue.

"A Snell? A Snell!" Crisha managed to speak twice before they reached the clear ground and she could really talk. Then she burst forth. "The last people you need to be having anything to do with around here are those Snells. Stay away from them. Don't you have any consideration for Charles? Poor trash is all they are. Poor trash."

Adrienne bristled at the prejudice. However, she had already learned that her indignations were in vain. Regarded as ignorance by the ignorant.

At evening dining Charles' foreman, Stewal, joined the family. The great future of the Double C was rehashed.

Adrienne listened with contentment.

A slightly mercenary city girl with a propensity for shopping malls, Adrienne liked to hear how rich she was about to become. It was an extra, something she had not counted on when she fell in love with Charles, thinking he was only another businessman being entertained by her boss in Houston. Now, more like an emperor than a rancher, Charles reigned at the head of the table, his cowboy hat casually tossed on the serving cart, chewing on his slender perennially unlit pipe.

Servants hovered nearby, ready to fulfill his every wish. Those at the table, with the possible exception of Crisha, knew they were there at his pleasure, knew he was master of land and money.

The foreman's daughter, Verna Mae, a lithe blue eyed brunette of sixteen, was quiet and shy almost to the point of intimidation, practicing the feminine submission still expected of 'good girls' in this area of the country.

The 1980s had yet to take hold in these parts of the United States.

Stewal, dusty and ragged, didn't remove his ten gallon hat until Crisha reminded him. Crisha, usually a huge somber machine, came alive, sending Stewal silent messages as the cowpoke conferred with Charles.

The strong build of the Welders that contributed to Charles' aura of infallible leadership had dealt Crisha a stunning blow. No matter how little fat she might have carried on her large frame she could never have appeared thin, an insurmountable negative in the eighth decade of the 20th century. Substantial extra weight made her loom colossal and masculine.

But in Stewal's presence she almost shrank with femininity.

It was at a previous meal of fried chicken and mashed potatoes, served by the trained help, eaten off a long unvarnished clothless table with sterling silverware and china plates, that Adrienne had decided to accept Charles' marriage proposal.

An army brat without any real home, she had come to Houston during the last recession's great rush for jobs in that city, With a Bachelor of Business degree she had landed a good position with an oil company and met Charles Welder during the course of business. Rich in oil and cattle, he was also an international businessman as well as a rancher.

Also a widower.

After a dizzying two month courtship in Houston, dotted with quick trips to his ranch, Charles formally proposed.

Impressed by a gallery of Welder ancestral photos hung in the ranch house's long hallway, Adrienne envisioned her portrait joining them, a permanent place in a family at last.

As easy as love at first sight it seemed, but marrying such a man was proving as complicated as merging corporations. At once Adrienne had to leave her job and come to the Double C to begin adapting to life in the huge ranch house located at the wooded western edge of three hundred thousand acres. Always a city girl, she was also a rough drive away from the small town of Effilville that had grown up nipping at the Double C's south flank.

As the meal drew to a close, Charles was gesturing emphatically to Stewal, hammering in some obscure point about cattle. Crisha's face strained with interest. Verna Mae stared in silence. Adrienne felt strangely cold as dessert materialized before her.

The sun was dropping behind the hills.

"Say, do you recall?" Adrienne interrupted Crisha's enrapture. "Did I have my sweater with me in the forest today? Or did I leave it somewhere else?"

"Darling." Charles abandoned Stewal abruptly. "Have you

been walking alone in those woods again?"

"No, I was with-"

"It's all right, Charles. I rescued her. More wine, Stewal? I'll get it for you myself."

Crisha laboriously rose and reached for a wine decanter but her fingers did not quite grasp it. It fell to the floor, spilling most of the red liquid.

"Butterfingers!" Crisha exclaimed, as a maid rushed to the spot with carpet cleaner.

"Charles," said Adrienne. "I must have some exercise and also I need some time to myself once in a while."

"You'll have plenty of exercise running this house. You're skin and bones anyway," said Crisha.

Adrienne frowned and rose from the table.

"You left your sweater on the porch," said Crisha, sternly as to a child expected to retrieve a misplaced article at once.

"Yes, of course. I'll get it."

Charles had not taken his eyes off Adrienne. His expression was unnervingly intense, but as she exited to the porch she heard his voice once again raised in friendly debate.

Adrienne eagerly gasped the cool night country air.

Such a treat, sharp and sweet. So pure. An anecdote to the fatigue of adjusting to the unfamiliar. As a Yankee in Texas ranchland, Adrienne sometimes felt more like an earthling on Venus.

Unless it was wintertime, Houston night air rarely became cold, only more humid and heavy.

Here in East Texas the heaviness was lifted like fog rising into a low cloud, cloaking the sky in an eerie mist.

The sweater was slung over an old rocker that gently creaked back and forth, back and forth. She picked it up and occupied the chair, holding the sweater close. The rocking soothed her. She leaned her head back and closed her eyes.

"Charles." A faint cry from the woods erased all thought of relaxation. Adrienne came stiffly to attention in the rocker.

"Charles." A desperate engulfing whisper.

Adrienne slowly turned her head as though she hoped to find

the setting sun in her visual path but was afraid to view its rays.

"Char- rels!" The whisper rose to a scream. A deathly inhuman scream.

Adrienne jumped up and spun around. The trees were silhouetted against the hills.

The blond phantom was coming across the clearing in a little trot, for her blue lace gown prevented an all-out run.

Anguish distorted her features. She held one hand to her face.

Rigid, Adrienne walked to the edge of the porch. The setting orange sun made spots before her eyes.

"Charles." The blue gown stopped swishing in the grass.

The plea was heartbreaking. Arms reached toward the house.

"Charles, it's Patricia. Why don't you come home to me?"

Terrified, Adrienne had a sharp vision of Charles succumbing to the desperate spirit. She imagined him running towards it, then the falling slowly to his knees as the evil leach sucked his life away.

Adrienne drew all the strength within her. "You cannot have Charles!" she shouted.

The golden curls resting on the blue laced shoulders bobbled back and forth. The arms fell in despair. "No, no, no!" Patricia insisted over and over. "I want Charles with me… with me… with me…"

"Adrienne?"

Charles was calling. She heard the tap-tap of his boots coming closer. Frantic, Adrienne whirled and threw herself against the back door.

"Wait, darling! I'm coming in!" She snatched the sweater and bolted in breathless, grasping him, holding him, preventing his exit onto the porch and the fate awaiting him there.

Moments later, safely inside, the great library doors closed behind Adrienne and Charles. Stewal and Verna Mae had long since gone home, Charles informed her. Crisha was nowhere in sight. Adrienne dropped all pretense of composure and collapsed shaking against the desk.

"Adrienne." Charles caught her. His grip was strong but his face as ambiguous as ever. She leaned against him gratefully.

Then, after a moment, she embraced him.

She said, calmly, "I won't let anything take you from me."

"What's happened? What is wrong?" He pushed her down in a large leather chair and stood opposite her.

She pinched the skin on her arm until it turned white. "I must know about your wife. You see-" she faltered, unable to explain. "I've heard ghost stories."

"Ghost stories? Darling, don't listen to ghost stories."

"How did she die?"

Charles rose and stood before his large wall of books, searching the titles as though in one he would find an answer.

He cleared his throat.

"What do you already know?"

"Only that she was your wife. And she was blond and beautiful."

"Oh, God she was beautiful."

Adrienne flinched at the longing in his voice,

"But-" Charles spoke normally again. "She had to die, I suppose."

"How?"

"Don't ask." Tears came to his eyes. Adrienne ran to him and found herself holding him, comforting him. "I could have helped her but I was too stubborn. I- She- she was a- suicide."

Adrienne grasped him tighter and they held one another for the longest time.

Nothing more could be said.

Suicide.

"She was evil, no good, trash." said Crisha, the next morning.

Adrienne and Crisha were walking among the animals in the yard at one of the Double C's huge barns.

Crisha picked up a newborn kitten and held it up in the air as though inspecting it. Then she tossed it up with a laugh as the animal squeaked with fright. Adrienne feared the baby cat would fall to the hard earth below. But Crisha managed to catch it and tossed it in the hay. It ran meowing loudly to its mother.

"She killed herself. That's all. Just poor trash. Charles

should've never married her."

Adrienne bit her tongue to keep from snapping at Crisha's annoying habit of referring to everyone she disliked as trash.

"How exactly did she die?"

Crisha gave Adrienne a 'you-asked-for-it-you-got-it-you-deserve-it' stare.

"She hanged herself in those woods you're so fond of tramping in. By the neck. From that old four trunked oak tree at the end of the trail."

Adrienne arrived early the next morning at edge of the forest path. Candy was already there.

"Are we looking for anything in particular?" said Candy, as Adrienne led the way, beating at the brush with a stick.

"No, we're just exploring. Anything suspicious, out of place that doesn't belong in the woods."

"Good thing I'm along, considering what you know about forests." Candy giggled impishly. "Yankee."

"You're the only one in this place with a sense of humor. An odd sense of humor, but humor nevertheless."

"Warped some people might say."

"Oh, Candy. At least I can laugh with you. What a relief you are."

"You look awful today. Want to tell me all about it?

"I saw Patricia."

Candy paled. "So you're telling ghost stories, too?"

"No, I saw her. What am I going to do, Candy?"

Candy became suddenly serious. "Do you love Charles enough to risk yourself for him?"

"I want to help him. This is evil and Patricia is behind it, I'm sure. He's in such torment whenever anyone mentions her name."

"That must be stopped," Candy said sternly. "He can't marry you with this unresolved. I swore I wouldn't ever gossip about what happened unless it was absolutely necessary and I guess it is."

"Please."

"I'll tell you the known facts. Patricia was very young when they married. She had a baby the first year.”

“What? A child?”

“You didn't even know that?” Candy sighed, then continued in a low somber voice. “Unfortunately the baby was congenitally impaired. She was not expected to live beyond early childhood. It was a great disappointment, not just for the parents but the entire community. Still she was taken home to be cared for as long as possible. When the baby was only four months, Charles took a business trip.

“The Sunday after Charles left, the child died. Much sooner than expected. Crib death it was said. Apparently Patricia was alone with the baby. It was the servants' day off and the baby nurse had gone to church. Crisha was out with Stewal. Patricia said she and the child had taken a nap together and the child didn't wake up.

“Charles returned. The baby was mourned and buried. About two weeks later the stories began. Ghost stories, ha. Gossip.”

“Gossip?”

“Yes, gossip. Raised in cities I don't think you yet understand what gossip can do in a small community. People said they heard the baby's ghost crying in the night. Crying for vengeance for its murder.”

“Murder?”

“Child abuse. People said Patricia killed the baby. Some said it was a mishap due to her youth and inexperience, others told tales not even that kind. Charles tried to suppress the stories but the more he tried the more they grew. He then attempted a different tactic. He had the child's body exhumed. An autopsy revealed an undetected indication the baby was smothered. Nothing was done. Charles was powerful enough that the county grand jury ruled accident.”

“Accident?”

“Then Charles went away. He stayed away a long time. But Stewal's engagement to Crisha brought him back. The evening he returned, Patricia was found hanging in the woods.”

“Stewal and Crisha were engaged?”

“Didn't you even know that? Afterwards the wedding was postponed.”

“Charles must have loved her very much.”

Candy nodded. "He did." Her eyes misted. "But Patricia's death was not his fault. Only you can make him see that."

"How?"

"By confronting and defeating the figure you saw in those woods. By putting the ghost stories to rest once and for all."

"I can do that," said Adrienne with only the slightest hesitation in her voice.

Candy bit her lip. "There might be danger. Real physical danger. And I'd hate to see anything happen to you, Yankee. I wish there were more control over the situation. Everybody has to make their own choices. You'll do the right thing."

"Thanks." Adrienne hesitated. "You're right. I have to face her. I have to show her I'm here now and Charles belongs to me now."

"Yes." Candy turned away and looked inexplicably sad.

That evening Charles was unusually unhappy. A quiet despair had overtaken him ever since their conversation in the library. Adrienne longed to reassure him but she kept still, biding her time. Crisha took Verna Mae into town for a shopping expedition.

Precious moments alone with Charles were cut short when Stewal arrived early for dinner.

Not much in the mood for conversation this evening, Charles found an excuse to go outside before the foreman got through the front door.

"Charles went out back, Stewal." Adrienne took his dusty hat.

"I'll wait here." He dropped down on the couch.

"Sure." She watched as he fetched his tobacco wad from his pocket. "Stewal, can I ask you a personal question?"

"I guess so, mam. As you're the boss's new lady."

"What about you and Crisha? Why aren't you married? I know you were engaged."

Stewal looked hard at the floor, pinched the wad of tobacco and slowly sucked it into his mouth.

"I intend to marry her. I almost have enough money to buy myself a pretty nice place and, you know, work for me. I just couldn't stand to leave the boss so soon after- after his wife died." Stewal cocked his head. "She was no good. But he's has been punishing himself cause he couldn't help her. And I just couldn't marry Crisha and you know, still work here. But maybe soon." There was a large bulge in Stewal's cheek. "Maybe soon be two weddings in the family."

After dinner, Adrienne was waiting by her window.

Waiting for a glimpse of blue lace.

Behind her came a tap on the door and icy fingers touched her heart.

"It's Charles. Can I come in?"

"Of course." Adrienne fumbled for a light.

"Why were you sitting in the dark?"

"Such a lovely night. Nice breeze, nice stars."

"Oh." He sank down on the soft mattress, his shoulders sloped.

She moved towards him but his look stopped her.

"I came to tell you. About her."

The icy hand on her heart.

He buried his fingers in the knotty spread. "How I killed her."

The hand squeezed her heart into. She dropped down beside him. Oblivious of her terror he went on.

"She was depressed. She had lost a child. I don't know how it happened. I just know she could never have harmed the baby on purpose. She was barely 18. We should have waited before marrying, waited before having children. I know the baby's death was an accident. She was the sweetest kindest, most wonderful person. Lively, witty- a joy. And with my help she could have gone on. She was a fighter. She would have licked it. She just needed my help."

He broke off, losing composure for a moment. "I didn't understand depression is like cancer of the mind. I had no idea how much attention its victims demand from those they love." He raised his anguished eyes to Adrienne's. "Do you know what I did to her?"

"You left her." Adrienne's hand gripped his arm. Tears spilled from her eyes.

"More than that. I was just so tired of gloom, of her blackness. I was still in my 20s. I wanted the happy funny girl I'd married back. I

129

decided I was going to provoke her out of it.

"She was standing before the window in our room, much as you stood when I came in. I called her name. She didn't answer. I had drank too much that evening. I called her again. No response.

"Then such a rage took hold of me, such anger and longing. I grabbed her by the shoulders and spun her around in front of me. I faced the mirror. As I raved, I could see my fingers digging into her bare shoulders, turning them blue. She was so small and her blond hair shaking against the back of her blue gown. I saw what I was doing it to her. Saw myself, my ugly distorted face towering over her, but I couldn't make myself stop.

" 'No, Charles', she pleaded with me, not understanding it was not the baby's death I was angry about. 'I didn't harm our baby. I was asleep when she died.'

" 'Do you know who you are?' I said. 'You are Mrs. Charles Welder now. Not some lower class living in town. Do you know what people are saying about you? The Double C has a reputation to maintain. I can't have people in this community thinking my wife's emotionally disturbed-'

" 'I'm trying.'

" 'By hell you will do more than try. You'll stand up straight and face it.' She had begun to cry and this infuriated me more. I wanted to shock some sense into her. All I saw before me was regression. Then I told her she was not a fit mother for my children. I called her trash."

"Oh, no," said Adrienne.

"Then I left. That's why she haunts those woods. She does. I've seen her, in the blue lace she wore that night. I've heard her crying."

Charles Welder sighed, a deep sign of pain at an uncorrectable sin and the relief at its confession.

"Now you know what is behind the ghost stories."

"Charles, she must be laid to rest."

"Laid to rest? How? I don't see how that can ever be. Adrienne, I wanted so much to have a life with you. I should have married you in Houston. Given up the ranch to Crisha and Stewal. Put her to rest? If only that could be."

Adrienne could think of nothing to say which would comfort him.

He left as he came, in despair, his boots tapping away down the hall.

Adrienne switched off the light and resumed her vigil at the window.

Her cheek in her palm and her elbow on the window ledge, with the soft night breeze sifting by her, Adrienne was half asleep when the faint cry started.

"Charles."

Jerking awake, Adrienne stared hard outside the window. Patricia's gown illuminated by moonlight, her face in darkness, was breaching the edge of the woods. Quickly, silently, Adrienne slipped out the bedroom, down the hall, down the stairs, to the back porch. Clutching a small flashlight, she leaned over the railing for a better look at the fire behind the smoke of the ghost stories.

Patricia was coming closer and closer. Arms again outstretched. "Charles. Charles," she breathed.

Adrienne let her come within twenty five feet of the porch steps. Then without any prior warning Adrienne flew down the steps and ran as hard as she could across the clearing.

Towards the ghost.

The figure in blue stopped short. Opened, then shut her mouth silently. Then the ghost screamed and turned and ran away.

Adrienne pursued, across the clearing, down the wooded path, past the four trunked oak. Not until she was almost physically upon the other, did she realize that the unearthly calls to Charles had evolved into very earthly screams indeed. As she wrestled blue lace to the ground, Adrienne was conscious of flesh, then both blood and flesh under her fingernails. She reached and snatched a blond wig off a brown head.

"Verna Mae?"

"You little fool."

Adrienne knew they were deep in the woods. Although she had the younger smaller girl firmly in hand, another stood over them.

Another had spoken of a fool. Adrienne turned.

Crisha stood, pointing a gun. "You little idiot, How could you let her get close enough to catch you? You've ruined everything."

"Crisha?" Adrienne was momentarily confused. Then the truth dawned. "You're behind the ghost stories?"

Crisha did not reply. She just snatched the young girl away from Adrienne and pushed her so violently aside that the teenager struck the ground again.

"Why?"

"Tell her why, Crisha."

Relief swept over Adrienne as she recognized Candy's genial voice behind Crisha.

Crisha gave a cry of terror and dropped the gun.

Candy picked it up and pointed it at Crisha.

"Tell her now."

"She is dead I tell you! I killed her myself." Crisha's massive figure became hysterical gelatin. "I put that rope around her delicate little neck myself and she hanged from this tree until she was dead, dead. Dead!"

Crisha beat the tree with her bare fist.

"Don't stop. Tell her why," Candy insisted, her voice strong and soft.

Crisha stood stock still. Her voice became sadly childish. "I didn't mean to hurt the baby. I just wanted to hold her, play with her, sleep with her." Crisha's eyes became vicious again. "She saw. I know it. She saw but she never said a word."

Adrienne saw.

Like sequential slides flashing before her eyes.

Clumsy Crisha sneaking into the room, taking the baby from beside her sleeping mother, bringing her into the den.

Awkward Crisha falling sleep next to the fragile infant, waking, realizing the child was dead, returning to the sleeping mother's arms a lifeless body.

Candy reached over and pushed Crisha. She went down like a flattened cardboard doll. Candy handed the gun to Adrienne.

"Watch them. I'll get the sheriff."

"How did you know I was going to need help?"

Candy glanced around. "Where's Charles?"

"At the house."

"Is he all right?"

"As far as I know. I just saw him before our 'ghost' appeared."

"Good," said Candy. "You heard the truth. Verna Mae will be your witness."

Adrienne stared in wonder at Crisha who was helpless on the thick carpet of leaves and pine needles. The Stewal girl was curled up, sobbing amidst a bush.

"You're a witness as well- Candy?"

Candy grasped Adrienne's hand with the familiar strong loving grip. Her natural beauty glowed.

"No more ghost stories," said Candy. "Charles must be freed from his guilt. Whatever human failings he displayed, he has suffered enough for them. Promise, no more ghost stories."

"Don't worry." Adrienne became aware of the strange concern Candy bore for Charles. "I promise."

"I've got to go. Watch them good until the sheriff gets here." She started towards the clearing then turned, smiling with encouragement. "The future is yours now, Yankee. You've laid the spirit to rest tonight. So remember that promise!"

Adrienne smiled back in happy triumph.

Charles and Adrienne sat at the massive maple table, the servants had vanished for the time being. They were alone.

Later she and Charles would be together in his bedroom, no longer watching for ghosts out the window.

But for the time being, they simply sat in the center of the table, the head chair empty, their two side chairs pulled close together so their hands could meet whenever the need arose.

Reflecting on the greed of the living, they ate little.

Easy to plant stories that the child was abused. Easy then to record a baby's cry and play it late at night.

As the stories about Charles seeing her ghost grew and strengthened, the climate would become ripe for him to 'commit suicide'. Crisha and Stewal would have had everything then.

The next night Adrienne and Charles embraced in his bed.

"I guess I can put this back." Charles reached and got an album from beneath the foot of the mattress, took out a loose photo and replaced it in the empty frame.

Adrienne rose and stood beside him.

Stewal was in Effilville, arranging a lawyer for his daughter, claiming that he knew nothing. Crisha, under medical restraint, had not yet become coherent enough to dispute him.

"Stewal was in on it all right," Charles declared to Adrienne. "Stewal knew that Crisha wasn't with him that night as she'd said. He figured out what had happened and used it for his own gain."

"And the ghost stories were planted by Crisha and Verna Mae," said Adrienne, staring at the photo.

"The 'ghost' came in handy to frighten you, and disrupt our wedding plans." Charles rose and stood at the foot of the bed. "I was so blind."

"You must stop blaming yourself."

"I don't think it's quite sunk in yet but I'm beginning to appreciate how different, how better my life, our lives will be now that we know."

"Infinitely better."

He smiled. "What made you sure the ghost was a fake?"

"I didn't. It was- my friend- Who I think I won't see any more." Adrienne reflected. "I'll miss her."

"I suppose it was obvious to everyone but an idiot like me. Will you mind the picture? I'd like to display it now."

"You should. It belongs with the rest of the family portraits. And don't put the album away." Adrienne reached.

Charles handed her the album.

Her fingers traced the embossing on the leather cover. 'Wedding album of Charles Carl Welder and Patricia Candace Snell'. Then underneath someone had scribbled in impish hand, 'Charlie and Candy!-the Double Cs'.

"It was so apt she went by her middle name, Candy," said

Charles. "She was ravenous for fine chocolates."

Adrienne turned the pages. At the very back of the book was a bittersweet picture of a frail infant in her mother's arms.

"We called the baby Angel," said Charles.

"Appropriate," said Adrienne. "Like her mother."

Charles took the album back. "This also can be put in a proper place with other genealogy records." He opened a bureau drawer and slipped it in. "Intact, but away. No more guilt."

That was Candy's desire, thought Adrienne.

And no more ghost stories.

The Simple Way

A Lieutenant Plate in Sand Waves Mystery Short Story

By Deborah DR Kralich

Location: Sand Waves, Texas, USA- an elite command design colony between Houston and Galveston.

Characters:

Lieutenant Sinclair Peter Plate- Young, attractive, intelligent second ranking officer among a handful in an elite Houston community.

Jeannie Daphne Martin- Attractive, intelligent successful life insurance agent cracking glass ceilings in the 80s.

M. Cecelia Holmes- 27-year-old oil production manager.

Carol E. Bagby- 28-year-old labor relations specialist.

Matt Powers- Oil company vice president with too many fiancés.

Officer Timothy Willhouse- One of those wiry, thirtyish men still capable of passing for 19.

Officer Grant Skaar- Stereotypical tall rugged looking Texas police officer.

Dr. Al Lutton- Prominent Sand Waves surgeon who knows his limitations.

Chief Robert Brecken- Conventional, competent administrator, he leaves the detecting to his talented subordinates.

Ms. Perkins- Described only as a gray-haired woman wearing glasses.

And **Ace Madison**- Detective extraordinaire space traveler, despite working only in outer space, he does his part for the earthly force in Sand Waves.

The Simple Way

by Deborah DR Kralich

Two striking women, a brunette in yellow silk and a blonde in blue taffeta, faced each other and squared off in the pale green hospital corridor.

"She did it," said the blonde, swishing her knee length dress with her left hand and pointing with her right. "She shot him."

"No." The brunette spoke not to her accuser but to the unhappy looking man positioned between them. "I did not shoot Matt. I couldn't. I loved him. She shot him."

The man in the middle, Lieutenant Sinclair Plate of the Sand Waves Police Department, sighed and stepped backwards. Giving into a strong urge, he leaned against the wall.

Like prizefighters hearing the bell, the two women started forward. Plate bounced off the wall and landed back between them just in time to prevent the first blows. The women silently retreated. Their eyes deadlocked as though each believed the first to break eye contact would be judged guilty.

Plate felt a bad headache coming on, having just arrived at the Sand Waves General Hospital where the victim, Matt Powers, an executive vice president with Houston Deep Drop Oil Drilling Equipment Company, had been brought in with a gunshot wound. Not alleviating his stress was the presence of Plate's own girlfriend, now thrust into the role of bystander. He and Daphne had met the previous November although their romantic relationship had not gone into full swing until after the first of the year.

New Year's party hats had not been stored away three weeks when the unfortunate Mr. Powers had suffered trauma with malice aforethought, making the 1983 celebration potentially his last.

Repeatedly passing each other to alternately tailgate the ambulance on the way to the hospital had been two nearly identical four-door brand new 1983 Bonnevilles, each one driven by one of the women Plate was now keeping physically apart.

Both women had jumped out of their Pontiacs and raced into the hospital emergency area, each screaming that Powers was her fiancé and that the other had shot him.

Hospital security had stood guard over the women until Plate was paged.

The security employee was lackadaisical about his job. Both women had visible scrapes from encounters he had enabled.

Plate banished Daphne to an adjacent waiting room and took over the security guard's position in the hospital corridor, separating the women. He gave the guard instructions to relay to two Sand Waves patrolmen on their way.

Suspect A - brunette, M. Cecelia Holmes, was an attractive 27 year old production manager with the Catwild Oil Company. She stated she had been seeing Powers for about six months. Cecelia knew he dated other women, suspect B among them, but recently had broken off with all others when he had chosen his one and only. Cecelia claimed he had given her an engagement ring early this morning. And she had a lovely ring flashing on the proper finger.

Suspect B - blonde, Carol E. Bagby, was a beautiful 28 year old labor relations specialist with the Fellstrike Oil Company. She had been seeing the victim for six months. Carol Bagby also said she knew he dated Cecelia Holmes. Carol stated that Powers had broken off with the brunette when he had decided to marry her. Carol claimed that Powers proposed that morning and had produced a ring which she had promptly planted on her finger and there it still was.

Both rings were identical.

Each claimed the other had burst into Powers' apartment to which each had a key. Each claimed the other had shot Powers, then she had jumped on her and they had struggled over the gun.

During the struggle both women had handled the gun, managed to fire a few more shots into the ceiling, and as such it was impossible to tell which had fired the shot that had wounded Powers.

Plate held his arms out, scarecrow fashion. The women were now stalking one another in circular clockwise movements, with Plate in dead center.

Plate pivoted to keep his arms a symbolic wedge between them, acutely aware one was actually innocent and suffering the prospect of a terrible loss.

The other was a dangerous sociopath.

While keeping the two women at bay, Plate yelled down the corridor to the 220 pound hospital security guard who was getting a snack out of the vending machine.

"Can I get your assistance here, please?"

The security guard bent over and pulled his Milky Way out of the slot and started in the direction of the waiting room.

Plate alternately looked back and forth between the two women who had been competing for the same man.

The security guard came back and relieved Plate of his role of prizefight referee, giving the detective a chance to explain to Daphne, still in the waiting room, observing much like a peeping tom from the doorway.

"One of them, the loser, had formulated a plan. A plan that had worked up to the point of the bullet impact. Powers is not dead but in critical condition with a head wound. Whether or not he will ever regain consciousness is still up in the air but if he does, one of those pretty fiancées of his is sunk." Plate pulled Daphne over the threshold back into the hall.

"What I'm noticing more than anything, is just how similar these two women are except for their hair color." Jeanne Daphne Martin, a 27-year-old career woman, was acutely aware of the common dress for success style utilized by virtually every woman her age in the corporate world competing in a predominantly male environment.

Compared to the suspects, her social peers, she was less heavily made up and dressed in a slim skirt, matching jacket and button-up blouse, and was nevertheless more classically lovely than the other two.

The fine line of her symmetrical facial structure was covered by silk smooth skin accented with baby blue eyes, moist pink lips, and framed with soft sunbeam yellow hair.

"Neither can compare to you," Plate commented, staring intently at his girlfriend.

Plate had been with Daphne at the posh Sand Waves Toy Museum Restaurant when reports of the shooting had disrupted their Saturday lunch. Daphne was accustomed to interruptions stemming from his job.

She didn't mind. In fact she savored them as long as she was able to tag along to the crime scene, always alert for an opportunity to do business.

Daphne was a life insurance agent, a very successful one. She was thrilled that, as long as she stayed discreetly in the background, Plate was more than willing to accept any assistance she could provide.

"All the expert detective work of the last two hours shows that one of them definitely shot him and one of them definitely did not," Plate had said. "So what is your analysis?"

"They are dressed similar in semi-formal clothing, not at all appropriate for this time of day or for either one of their jobs. The wounded man must have planned something special with the real fiancé for her to be dressed that way and the rejected woman knew about it and followed suit."

"Go on."

"I note that despite a few scuff marks here and there, both women could have come right out of a symphony concert as far as their appearances go," Daphne had replied. "Neither had more than 7 hairs out of place, and the only real sign of trauma is their makeup is ruined by their tears."

"Powers had indeed chosen between them and purchased an engagement ring for one of them," reported Officer Willhouse, as he and Officer Skaar arrived in the hospital corridor.

"We visited Ridgway Jewelry, following the instructions we

got from you via the security guard," said Willhouse.

"Powers bought an engagement ring," said Skaar. "He's a regular at Ridgway jewelers, likes to give his girlfriends lots of baubles. And there's been lots of girlfriends in the past, said the jeweler. Also managed to speak to his boss at the oil drilling company. The boss confirmed that, while Powers has few male acquaintances, there's been plenty of women over the years. According to his boss, apparently in the last six months he had narrowed it down to two. He told his boss he was ready to settle down but out of deference to the rejected party, he wanted to keep it quiet for the moment. Apparently, according to our interviews, Powers had not revealed the choice to any of his business associates or friends and he has no family. Everybody said he was the type of guy who would try to minimize embarrassment to the rejected woman as much as he possibly could. The boss had no idea which woman had come out on top."

"But," said Willhouse, taking up the narration. "This is what the jeweler told us-

"It was the day after Mr. Powers had purchased a $12,000 diamond. A woman came in identifying herself as Powers' secretary had come in asking for an identical ring.

" 'I am on a rather delicate mission for my employer, Mr. Powers,' the lady had told the jeweler. Now the jeweler describes this woman as thin with a nice figure, wore glasses. She had grayish hair, that yes, could have been a wig. And the glasses she wore were sunglasses. She had Powers' MasterCard with her, the same card he had used the previous day to pay for the first ring. When he saw the card, the jeweler said he panicked that Powers was dissatisfied with the original ring, and was sending the secretary to return the ring.

" 'There is no dissatisfaction. On the contrary, Mr. Powers wants a second identical ring to this one,' the secretary had explained. 'The second ring is for Powers' mother, an elderly lady all alone in the world except for her son, Mr. Powers. She is feeling a little left out with the preparations underway for the first marriage of her only boy. I implore you to exercise complete discretion in the matter as Mr. Powers had judged it a sound idea not to tell his fiancée about

Mother's little problem and he is acutely embarrassed at having to do so. His psychological counselor did recommend that purchasing an identical ring for his mother would go a long way to soothing her feelings and stopping her from becoming an impediment to the marriage. He is most embarrassed about this and would prefer to never hear it mentioned,' the jeweler told me the woman said to him."

"Moreover," said Skaar, as Willhouse paused to catch his breath. "The next day the secretary returned to pick up the ring. She had brought cash explaining Powers had decided not to charge the purchase after all. His psychologist had made a special visit to his office to impress upon him that it was imperative that his fiancée not find out about the ring purchased for his mother until after the wedding. The jeweler had nodded understandingly and winked. That night the jeweler had gone home to his wife and told her there were all kinds in the world. Whether or not the ring was really for Powers' mother was a good question and he didn't care."

"Of course, Powers' mother died years ago," said Willhouse.

"I have to get back to my rounds," the security guard called out.

"Obviously the potential killer had intended to kill both Powers and the victorious bride-to-be," suggested Daphne. "Then the loser would pose as the winner, claim the other had killed Powers, and she killed the other woman in self-defense after Powers was shot."

"That plan went haywire when the real fiancée fought back and while she may not have won, she didn't lose either. Now to top it off, Powers might not die," said Plate. "Hang on a few more minutes could you please?" he said to the security guard, then spoke back to Daphne and his patrolmen again. "One of those beauties has to be sweating it out underneath."

"Lieutenant Plate, I got here as fast as I could."

Plate looked up into the face of the police chief, Robert Brecken. He led the chief to the two suspects and their respective police guards. Daphne followed demurely.

"Ms. Holmes, Ms. Bagby," said Plate, as he relieved the security guard. Plate addressed the two simmering women suspects as his chief followed him. "May I present my supervisor, Chief Brecken?"

"Ladies," said Chief Brecken, inclining his head a little as he acknowledged them.

For a moment suspects A and B simultaneously abandoned pursuit of one another and gaped at the chief who was dressed in colorful Bermuda shorts and a bright red shirt.

Officer Willhouse, one of those wiry, thirtyish men still capable of passing for 19, stood at attention. Officer Skaar, stereotypical tall rugged looking Texan, took a second look or two and stepped back, his hands clasped behind his back.

"Skaar," said Brecken, tapping him on the shoulder, holding out his palm. "The paperback."

Officer Skaar tried passing the novel to Daphne. But it was too late. The chief had seen the book.

"How many times do I have to tell you, no reading on duty?" said Plate to Skaar in a firm, yet not unfriendly tone of voice.

"Sorry, sir."

"Skaar, Willhouse, each of you take one of those ladies to a separate waiting lounge while I confer with the chief."

"Yes, sir."

"Yes, Lieutenant."

"Skaar reading on duty again. I thought I had put a stop to that," said the chief, as Skaar and Carol Bagby disappeared around the corner.

"Well, he says it helps him in his police work," said Plate, watching Willhouse and Cecelia Holmes fade into the opposite direction. "I have, on occasion, found reading fiction useful as well."

Plate took the paperback from Brecken and read from the cover. " 'Another amazing story of *Ace Madison, Space Traveler. Episode 29- The City Eating Monster of Venus.*' "

"Well, Plate," Brecken said. "Let's concentrate on earth villains right now. I was briefed on the way over. Which one do we put our money on?"

"I don't know."

"What you mean you don't know? You always know. Good

afternoon, Ms. Martin. I know it won't surprise you if I say that I'm not surprised to see you here."

"Good afternoon, Chief." Daphne almost whispered.

"Honestly, I don't know," said Plate. "It's going to take a while, even with, um, Daphne's assistance."

The other man looked at Daphne with consternation. "Plate, do you remember what day tomorrow is? Or should I say today is? The first day of my first vacation since I contracted with the Sand Waves Community Association to head this police department. And do you know what time it is? 2 PM. And you know what time my plane leaves? 7:30 PM. You may want time off for a good reason some day. A police convention, vacation. Honeymoon."

Daphne jumped. Plate remained impassive.

"I'm sorry, chief, but I still don't know." With a deft movement Plate flipped through the pages. "I haven't read this masterpiece yet. Maybe the answer is in here." He opened the book near the last chapter and read aloud.

" 'The police had the monster surrounded. But on the other side of the monster, an identical monster was brought in by the Venus Bureau of Investigation. How could Ace Madison determine which monster had eaten the city of Platego? And which monster was innocent?

'Nomedoit,' said one monster, vehemently in Venetian.

'Himdoit,' said the other monster, pointing at his rival.

Madison had a difficult problem on his hands. Both the city police and the VBI were looking to him for the ultimate answer.' "

"Excuse me."

Plate stopped reading. Daphne stepped further back.

The chief folded his arms.

"I was told by hospital security that I could find a captain and a lieutenant here from the Sand Waves Police Department." The man was eyeing them dubiously, casting a glance at Daphne on the periphery. "I am Dr. Lutton, chief surgeon at this hospital."

Sure enough, he wore a name tag on his breast- 'Dr. Al Lutton'.

"I am Chief Brecken."

"Lieutenant Plate."

The doctor shook hands with both men. Plate held the still opened paperback, bookmarked with his thumb. He glanced down at it and back up at the doctor several times as the conversation continued.

"I thought you might like a progress report on the patient."

"Go ahead." Chief Brecken had spoken.

Plate had jumped to the ending of the book.

"Plate, the doctor has a report on the condition of our victim. You know, the shooting victim. The one here on earth."

"Right," said Plate, bookmarking the paperback with his thumb again. "What can you tell us?"

"In order to best serve the patient's needs he will have to be transported to the medical center in Houston. I've consulted with three other doctors on this and we agree. Our intensive care unit does not have the sophisticated technology this patient will need. We are just an urban hospital."

"Right!" Plate shouted at the doctor causing him to step back. "We do want a report on the victim. But we need to wait about 10 minutes or so. Would you meet me in front of the lounge down the hall in 10 minutes?"

"I beg your pardon?"

"Doctor, I need to continue this conversation in just about 10 minutes."

Chief Brecken gave Plate an 'are you nuts?' look but did not contradict him.

"Chief, get Willhouse and Skaar. Have them bring the suspects into a waiting room and stay with them. Daphne, stand by. I will tell you what I need you to do."

Brecken and Daphne did as Plate asked.

"Doctor, let me explain." Plate took Dr. Lutton's arm and led the puzzled physician the opposite direction. He called to Chief Brecken over his shoulder, "if this works you will get to catch your plane."

"I'll just assume you know what you're doing as always," muttered Brecken.

Ten minutes later all the policemen, the two suspects, Daphne, and Dr. Lutton were in the same hallway.

"So, Doctor," said Plate, loudly. "You were about to give me a report on Powers' condition."

"Yes, I was. I'm happy to inform you that Mr. Powers has regained consciousness."

Both women had to be held back by their respective guards. Willhouse and Skaar admonished the suspects to remain quiet.

"Excellent. Then I must see him at once."

"I'm afraid that's out of the question. His condition is such that it is imperative that we get him to the medical center as soon as possible. Life Flight has been called. And they are sending a technician to determine if Powers qualifies as a bona fide emergency and to prepare him for the trip. If he does, which I'm confident he will. As soon as Ms. Perkins arrives and certifies him, the helicopter will be on its way."

"Before she gets here, just five to ten minutes with Powers. Just two minutes."

"I'm afraid I cannot allow anyone to see Powers. He is still in critical condition. His life is still very much in danger. However, I do believe he will live but he is fragile. We don't want him upset. So I must refuse your request."

"Doctor," said Brecken, "perhaps you don't understand. This man alone knows who shot him. Unless the he is able to identify his assailant before he dies, we will not be able to prosecute his murderer."

"Chief Brecken, I am not concerned with the technicalities of the police profession. This man is my patient. I expect him to live."

"Then may I at least post a guard at his door?"

"You may do anything you want out here in the hall. You can have a whole troop of police come in. But I will have a nurse stationed in Powers' room with firm instructions to admit no one except a gray haired woman wearing glasses. Ms. Perkins, the Life Flight representative."

"Your lack of cooperation will be duly noted, Dr. Lutton," said Plate.

"You can duly note on a French horn for all I care." Dr. Lutton strode off angrily down the hallway.

"Damn!" said Brecken. "We've no alternative but to let those two in there go. Skaar. Willhouse."

Both suspects were pulled forward by their guarding officers.

"Ladies, I'm going to have to let you go. But as you are both citizens of Sand Waves, we know where you are. It is obvious that one of you shot Matt Powers but as there is no way of telling which at the moment. This matter will have to wait until later. And apparently so will my vacation."

The suspects walked out of the hospital and went their separate ways.

A short time later in the darkened room where a patient lay, attended by nurse, a woman tapped lightly on the door. Officer Skaar stood outside the door. Or to be more precise he was leaning against the wall outside of the hall where Matt Powers' room was, reading another paperback, *Auction of Worlds*, another book by Carl S. Kralich.

A gray-haired woman carrying what looked to be a briefcase, dressed in a brown linen suit with glasses, walked by Officer Skaar, who barely glanced up from his paperback, and knocked on the hospital room door. The nurse softly cracked open the door.

"I am Ms. Perkins, the Life Flight attendant."

"I've been expecting you," said the nurse.

"I'll need to examine the patient in privacy."

"Naturally. While you're with him, I'll just get some coffee."

"Fine."

As soon as the nurse was outside, the attendant bent over Powers' silent form and appeared to check his breathing.

She reached into her pocket and extracted a sharp steel nail file, raising it over Powers' chest.

But before she could finish her strike, Lieutenant Plate had one arm around her waist and the other clasping her wrist, restraining the hand holding the file. Then she twisted the woman's arm behind her back, grasped her hair and pulled. The wig came off.

147

Brown hair brushed her cheek.

"Ms. Holmes," said Plate he whispered softly in her ear as she stiffened. "I have been expecting you."

"Now," said Plate to Daphne, Willhouse, and Chief Brecken, as they exited the hospital into the night air. "Powers is on his way to Houston in an ambulance. He is going to live but it's going to be several more days before he will be able to talk. But we've got the right one. Chief, you can catch your plane with a good conscience."

"I can't believe you pulled that off, Plate."

"It was easy. All I had to do was give the good doctor the lines to say. And make sure both suspects heard them. Everyone knows of Life Flight, but how many people understand their procedure? How many would know whether or not they would have an attendant come out and verify the emergency? And remember the state of mind of the guilty party. Knowing that she might go to prison for a long time if Powers talked. It was a wide open trap and she fell right into it. We put a mannequin in the bed. Daphne volunteered to play nurse. I hid in the restroom. Skaar pretended to be engrossed in his book."

"It is a really good book," said Skaar. "And I'm glad it was not the suspect I was guarding. Willhouse loves to arrest people more than me."

"All I had to do was grab her the minute she came in the room and raised her arm, showing her weapon."

"Keeping the lights dim in the room should have given her a clue that it was a trap," said Daphne. "They never turn the lights down on a patient who has not regained consciousness yet. But she didn't know any more about hospital procedures then she did about emergency transport procedures."

"I kind of suspected it was Holmes."

"What makes you say that?"

"Skaar, you said when you took Carol Bagby to the waiting room she was quiet and somber, as if what had happened was just sinking in. Whereas Willhouse said that Cecelia Holmes was real hyper, and made a big to do over how much in love she was with Powers. I'll take stunned silence over nervous chatter as a sign of innocence anytime. And I'm always suspicious of a woman who emphasizes over and over how much she loves a man."

"Yeah, there's a catch there somewhere." Daphne cut her eyes at him.

Plate looked at her and frowned.

"You did a good job, Plate, you and Skaar and Willhouse. A little extra help from our insurance agent amateur detective. Irregular as usual but it worked. I'm off on my vacation without a worry in the world."

"Listen, with diligent clue finding, mind exercising, and hard police work we could eventually have fingered the brunette. But chief, you were in a hurry. So I did it the simple way."

"Only you could have dreamed that scenario up."

"No," said Plate, producing Skaar's original paperback. "It was all here in *The City Eating Monster of Venus*. See, they had two monsters, identical, one good, one bad. And they had to tell which one ate the city and which one didn't eat the city. So they set a trap. They gave them a fake opportunity to munch on another city. They let them loose, and sure enough, the bad monster tried to take a bite out of the suburb and the good monster just went home."

After a pause, Daphne said, "you've finished? That's it?"

"That's it. Ace Madison got his man, um, monster. The simple way."

Published by Ruskras Corner

Humorous Futuristic Murder Mystery
by Deborah Denise

A Cat Whisperer– A Tale of felines, vampire, romance, murder, and mystery in the bizarre future soon to come.

Historical Murder Mysteries & Literature Fiction
by Deborah DR Kralich

The Mystique Woven in Our Land – set in 1792. The unlikely combination of witchcraft and high treason lead to treachery and murder, haunting a hero's daughter and the soldier she loves.

Murder as the Organist Plays – set in 1904. As the wedding music starts, the bride begins her long walk to the arms of her groom. She will not finish the journey. The beautiful bride emerges stunned, blood on her dress. She stands alone, blood dripping from a dagger at her fingertips. Unknowing, his back to this scenario, the organist plays on...

Interlude of Carelessness– set in the 1930s. An aristocratic German-American becomes a Texas police officer and falls in love with an Italian-American shop girl in 1930s Houston.

A Spy Come to Town– set in the 1950s. An international spy returns home to East Texas and becomes entangled with Texas Rangers on a local mystery involving his own family.

The Mystery of the Missing Persons– set in the 1960s. The turbulent 60s viewed from the eyes of a child who is writing her first mystery book.

Young Adult Science Fiction Series
by Carl S. Kralich

3748 A.D. The Return of the Cat– *A Karl Sabers Space Knight Adventure*. Talking cat aids a space hero and his princess girlfriend.

Auction of Worlds– *A Karl Sabers Space Knight Adventure.* Unlikely adventurer with cat seeks the empress sister of a royal alien beauty.

"Humorous young adult science fiction. Hilarious tale of princesses, pirates and a talking cat. For adults and young adults, male and female. Romance and gallantry in the stars," according to one review.

Lt. Plate in Sand Waves Mysteries
by Deborah DR Kralich
A series of traditional mysteries set in the 1980s including:

An Innovative Murder for the Season – At a small specialty store in a high-income community, a dozen or so people are trapped for 3 days and 2 nights. On the surface most appear to be strangers caught at random. Then there is a murder and it turns out the only real stranger among them is a detective whose presence is hardly coincidental.

The Ruler of the Toys– Intolerance and prejudice are major factors in the murder of an innocent woman who should have been without an enemy in the world. Before he can expose the masquerade of the killer, Lt. Plate has to uncover and understand deep dark secrets of long vanished eras.

A Kaleidoscope of Masquerades– Climatic events at a 1983 masquerade ball are merely the beginning of a kaleidoscope of confusion and anarchy that threatens life and liberty of a society facing change and choices that will reverberate into the future known as now.

The Unknown Puppeteer– On the eve of their marriage, Lt. Plate and Daphne must uncover a ruthless murderer or forfeit their chance for happiness for all time.

Short Stories featuring Lt. Plate:

Poised Like a Knife– included in the anthology of the same name. A hurricane threatens Sand Waves and murder coincides.

The Simple Way– included in the anthology titled *Poised Like a Knife.* An indecisive romeo finally chooses between two fiancees and the loser murders him. But which one was the reject out for revenge?

Poetry– *I Lift Up My Heart*– a book of Christian poetry
By Deborah DR Kralich

Available on Amazon and Kindle